ROGUE CYBORG

INTERSTELLAR BRIDES® PROGRAM: THE COLONY - 6

GRACE GOODWIN

Rogue Cyborg: Copyright © 2018 by Grace Goodwin

Interstellar Brides® is a registered trademark
of KSA Publishing Consultants Inc.

All Rights Reserved. No part of this book may be reproduced or transmitted in any form or by any means, electrical, digital or mechanical including but not limited to photocopying, recording, scanning or by any type of data storage and retrieval system without express, written permission from the author.

Published by KSA Publishers
Goodwin, Grace
Rogue Cyborg, Interstellar Brides®: *The Colony Book 6*

Cover design copyright 2019 by Grace Goodwin, Author
Images/Photo Credit: Deposit Photos: doodko, Angela_Harburn

Publisher's Note:
This book was written for an adult audience. The book may contain explicit sexual content. Sexual activities included in this book are strictly fantasies intended for adults and any activities or risks taken by fictional characters within the story are neither endorsed nor encouraged by the author or publisher.

GET A FREE BOOK!

JOIN MY MAILING LIST TO BE THE FIRST TO KNOW OF NEW RELEASES, FREE BOOKS, SPECIAL PRICES AND OTHER AUTHOR GIVEAWAYS.

http://freescifiromance.com

INTERSTELLAR BRIDES® PROGRAM

YOUR mate is out there. Take the test today and discover your perfect match. Are you ready for a sexy alien mate (or two)?

VOLUNTEER NOW!
interstellarbridesprogram.com

1

Makarios Kronos of Rogue 5, The Colony, Fighting Pits

RAGING, lust-soaked warriors faced one another in the fighting pits below. Sitting next to me in the stands, Warlord Braun pulled one hundred credits from his pocket and tossed the money to a large Prillon male seated three rows below us.

"Hey, Stone. One hundred on the Atlan, Tane."

The others called him Stone due to his complete lack of facial expressions. No emotion whatsoever. I could relate. The man was more machine than male, but I was not one to judge. I was a monster, even when compared to him.

Stone nodded and entered the data onto the tablet in his hand. The betting had begun hours ago, the moment the Prillon warrior bellowing in the pits issued his initial challenge. Seven warriors had answered his call. The tournament was set to begin. Eight cyborgs would fight until one remained. Eight would become four. Four, two. And the final two would fight to the end for the ultimate prize.

A battle, to the death if necessary, where the winner was granted the right to claim the female Gwendolyn of Earth as his own. She was a beauty. A woman warrior. Her body was toned and strong yet curved. My fingers would twitch with the need to reach out and touch her every time she walked near me. Her gaze was unrelenting, full of challenge, a challenge many warriors here were eager to answer. Like me and Stone, she barely showed emotion. No, that wasn't true. She showed emotion: anger, rage, fury, disdain. A female like her should smile, her eyes should show happiness. I'd give my right nut to hear her laugh. Fuck, to hear her scream in pleasure. She'd most likely had none since her arrival here —sexual or otherwise—like so many of us. She'd been a soldier before she was taken by the Hive. Before she was integrated. Changed.

Dark hair fell in waves down her back. It shimmered in the light and looked soft. I imagined wrapping my fist around it and holding her in place as I...

Fuck. No. I stopped the thought before my cock could respond. That way lay destruction. For both of us, even if I wanted to be the one to give her... feelings. Feelings besides the kind that roiled in your gut, churned and burned until there was nothing left.

Braun clapped me on the shoulder, breaking me from my thoughts. "Why are you not in the pit, my friend?"

"After you," I quickly countered, raising my hand as if to direct him down to the central fighting area for his own turn.

The Atlans here had adopted me as one of their own, but even they didn't know my secret, the truth behind why I wasn't going down there to beat the shit out of those eight males. To claim what I wanted with an ache in the vicinity of my heart—and definitely my balls—that hadn't gone away since I first laid eyes on her. *Gwen.*

But the truth wasn't something easily understood. It was the reason I could never dare take a mate for my own. And true, my ancestral world of Forsia, and Braun's planet, Atlan, were considered pseudo-cousins, orbiting in neighboring sectors of space, but I wasn't truly—or completely—Forsian. No, I was born on Rogue 5, making me the ruthless combination of part Hyperion animal and Forsian warrior. I might look similar in size to Braun and other Atlans, but that was where the similarities ended. My Hyperion/Forsian bloodline was so rare that officially, my kind didn't exist. As far as I knew, there were only three of us alive. All male. All unmated. All destined to die alone. Never father children. Which was a blessing. I would not wish my existence on an enemy, much less a son.

The last half-breed monster on Rogue 5 who'd tried to take a mate had accidentally killed her during their official claiming. The unique venom in our bite had entered her bloodstream and she'd died in his arms, unable to separate because his mating cock had grown within her and locked them together. Her body and her blood, infected by the poison unique to our rare mixed heritage, hadn't been able to adapt. She'd died and he'd wasted away, destroyed from within by guilt and self-hatred.

Despair. He'd known the possibility of killing her existed, but the urge to bite, to claim... to mate, had been too strong. He'd taken a chance and lost everything.

No. I would never claim a mate. Never fit in. Never belong. Not on Rogue 5 among my legion, the Kronos. Not on Forsia, where I wasn't wanted. Not here, on The Colony, among my exiled Atlan cousins. I was happier alone, on my trading vessel, wandering the stars as I'd done for most of my life.

Until the traitor caused my capture by the Coalition Fleet. My chest rumbled with the usual rage and heads turned my way. A quick, slicing glance had them turning away, eyes back on the pit.

Fucking traitor. When I found him...

If being handed over to the fucking Coalition hadn't been enough, they'd had shit for deflection shields and the entire fucking ship had been captured by the Hive while I rotted in the brig. But the Hive didn't care who was on board, Coalition fighters or Rogue 5 smugglers like me. We were all biological assets to be tortured and turned, assimilated into their war. Made into mindless drones. With me and a few others, they'd almost succeeded. Hell, with many, they had. We'd been the lucky ones to escape. Lucky ones to spend the rest of our existence here on The Colony, changed. Partially integrated and living in exile. Trapped. Trapped living on the same Colony base with the only female I'd ever wanted, but couldn't have.

Braun chuckled, his rumbling laughter pulling me from the darkness of my thoughts. His massive frame shook with amusement. "They are fools. They are fighting over a human female, but they know nothing of how to win her heart."

"And you do?" I asked.

Braun, Tane and I were the only survivors from that Coalition ship. Three out of over two hundred. Alive, but contaminated. Our torture and escape bonded us as brothers, despite the fact that we came from different worlds.

Everyone on The Colony assumed I was just an over-sized Atlan who maintained ruthless control, never going into beast mode. I wasn't an Atlan. I did not lose control or transform into a beast. No, my loss of control was more intimate, but every bit as life threatening to any female unlucky enough to ride my cock.

Braun and Tane had not felt the need to enlighten the rest of the warriors here about my true origins. Only the governor and the doctors knew that I wasn't Atlan at all, which suited me just fine. The less they knew, hells, the more they believed I could turn into a huge, raving killer at any moment, the better.

Braun was smiling now, his look almost wistful. "I have watched the governor and Ryston with their mate, Rachel. I have watched Hunt and Tyran with Kristin. The Everian Hunter with the human female, Lindsey. Caroline with Rezz. I watch all of them with their human mates, and I learn." Braun waved his hand at the eight warriors facing off in the arena, speaking among themselves, deciding on an order for battle. Rules. Ridiculous since they were all ready to kill each other for a female who had shown no interest in any male on the planet. "Gwendolyn will refuse them all. Even our brother, Tane. His victory will be empty."

"Tane will not win," I added, referring to the fight, not gaining Gwen's hand. "They will attempt to cripple him with their rules, refuse him the right to fight as a beast."

If a female was the prize, however, the rules would be forgotten the moment the challenge began. Apparently, Braun thought similarly and said, "A beast does not follow the rule of others. He will win."

I leaned back, assessing the warriors before us in the dirt arena. None of them were fucking good enough for Gwen.

Not one, not even Tane. I hoped Braun was right, that she would refuse them all, regardless of the victor, and hopefully before one of them died. She didn't need to be haunted by a death match as well as the implants left in her body by the Hive.

"So, my friend, if you truly watch the human females, what have you learned?" Curiosity made me ask. That was all.

He gave a small grunt and I wasn't sure if it was frustration or crankiness. "Human females like to believe they are independent. A mate must protect his Earth female without her realizing he does so."

"Why?" I asked, confused. "It is a mate's duty and right to protect his mate."

He held up his hand. "To claim a human female, a warrior must be very careful, plan well ahead. They are fierce and fearless mates. They will charge into battle against the Hive if they feel the need to protect their mate or children. They are too brave for their small, soft bodies. Too fierce for their own good," he practically growled. "They are fragile in body, but strong in will. They will risk too much, yet love completely. They are truly a mystery. Wild. Passionate. They need very strong, patient males to tame them."

Yes, that was the word. Tame. Gwen needed someone to tame her. Soothe her. Fuck her into oblivion so all her worries were gone. "And you want to tame Gwendolyn?" I was afraid of his answer but knew the truth. All males on The Colony wanted her. Lusted after her. Craved her.

Braun nodded, his gaze on the first fight beginning below. "Who would not?" Braun's smile was all hungry male. "She is magnificent. I will fuck her until she screams my name so many times, all other words have been forgotten."

It seemed our thoughts were aligned on many things. I doubted he was the only other male to imagine fucking her. Claiming her. Filling her tight pussy with his seed so she was marked. His and his alone. If I did it, she would most likely die. For anyone else on The Colony, she would have nothing but pleasure.

Fuck. I could not deny my friend his desires.

"She's a cyborg," I said. "A warrior. She will not be like the other human mates, the perfectly matched Interstellar Brides who came directly from Earth through the testing center instead of a Hive prison. She will be different." I pointed out the obvious, not because I thought her anything less than perfect, but because I didn't dare admit my interest aloud.

Braun lifted a brow in disgust and looked at me. "Do you insult the female?" The growl of his beast was in his voice, the bones of his face shifting under the skin as he fought off beast mode.

I shook my head. "No."

"Good. Do not." He instantly calmed. Braun didn't say, *she's mine*, but he warned me off all the same. The monster within me rose in answer, but I held onto control with an iron fist, giving nothing away. I had no rights over the female. Never would. Nothing could change that. Better a good male, like Braun, win her than another, lesser male. I would do my best not to hate him for touching her. Braun had been through hell and back. Tortured. Survived. He deserved happiness. If not on Atlan, then here, on The Colony. The planet for outcasts and the contaminated. The forgotten and fallen warriors from the Hive war.

Since Prime Nial, the ruler of Prillon Prime and commander of the Coalition Fleet, had lifted the ban on the contaminated returning to their home worlds, a few had chosen to leave The Colony and return to their old lives as best they could. The Prillons and Viken, the Trion and Everian, all could return home. But the humans here were not welcomed back on Earth with their Hive enhancements. That planet barely believed the Hive even existed. The governments wanted no proof of the merciless alien terror walking among their people. Never had I heard of leaders so afraid to speak the truth.

The Atlans could not return home either, their terrifying mating fever and beast mode too unpredictable. Normally, an Atlan was damn hard to kill. Filled with Cyborg tech, they were killing machines. The risk to their people on the home world would be too great should one go into mating fever and lose control of his beast.

And me? I knew my legion on Rogue 5 would take me in with open arms, but our leader, Kronos, would put me to use. He was nothing if not practical, and a Hive enhanced Forsian descendant would be the most terrifying weapon he would have. He would not hesitate to use it. Use me. And that was why I'd lived roaming space on my trading vessel instead of settling onto any specific planet. Until now.

I didn't kill on demand.

I didn't fight or steal on demand.

I didn't fuck on demand, either.

I owed none but Kronos a shred of loyalty, and even that had come at too high a cost.

I was here, still paying it. I ran my ship fast and hot, avoiding Hive and Coalition forces alike, getting Kronos what he needed from all corners of the galaxy. Until now.

Someone had given the Coalition news of my imminent arrival, and notice of the precious load of transport tech and weapons I'd been carrying. The Coalition's newest designs, and some illegal rifles manufactured on a non-Coalition world were among my cargo.

Guess it was the rifles that got me into that Coalition brig. And a captive of the Hive. And now, still a prisoner on The Colony, left to rot for decades, work in the mines, and die. The governor, a hard-ass named Maxim, wouldn't even allow me to leave the surface, go on a single mission off planet. He was afraid I'd escape.

He was right. But nothing he did would stop me. I simply waited for the right set of circumstances to arrive. The plan I'd had in place for weeks.

Despite Governor Rone's wishes, I refused to take a mate, to be tested for a bride. The truth was my own, my curse. I respected his frustration with me but was unable to comply with his demand that I mate. I just wanted to get back into space and mind my own fucking business. To be free, unchained to anyone or anything.

Taking a mate and leaving her behind? Not possible. The very idea made me growl again, the sound masked by the roar of the spectators as the first fight began and a Prillon in the pit landed a hard blow to his opponent. No, I was a smuggler, a rogue, a rebellious male who refused to follow commands, but I was not without honor. Even if our official claiming wouldn't physically kill her, I refused to hurt a female's tender heart in such a way.

A female was not just a huge risk, but a liability I couldn't afford.

The governor and the rest of the Coalition leadership had decided I was too unstable. Too much of a menace. Rogue 5. Hyperion. Forsian. Cyborg. I was a fucking freak among freaks. And the governor believed only a mate would calm me, anchor me to this planet and their war against the Hive. Ensure my loyalty to the Coalition cause.

But I was not Coalition born. I was Rogue 5. And I truly was a prisoner on this planet. Which made it hard to be grateful. Some days, I would have preferred to be dead, the need to escape making me feel like I was coming out of my skin.

The crowd roared and I turned my attention to the fighting pit once again. The large Prillon warrior was being hauled away unconscious as another stood with his arms raised in sweaty victory. The winner stepped aside and two fresh fighters entered the center of the ring. One, an Atlan I knew well. The other a Prillon warrior who was about to get his head broken.

"Smash him, Tane!" Braun's bellow was easily heard above the crown and our friend, Tane, looked up briefly and lifted his head in acknowledgement of Braun's encouragement.

"You cheer for him, but believe his fight is futile?"

Braun was grinning, leaning forward, his gaze glued to the fight as Tane lifted the Prillon over his head and threw him halfway across the fighting grounds. The Prillon rolled to his feet and screamed a challenge in return, the sound echoing off the stands, rushing at the Atlan with cyborg enhanced speed. He scored a solid strike at Tane's neck, although it barely shook the large Atlan. "Tane will win this fight and Gwen will refuse his claim. Once that is done, he will not protest my attempts to woo her."

I chuffed out a laugh and stared wide-eyed at my friend. "Woo her? What kind of word is that for a warrior? You sound like an old female."

The corner of his mouth tipped up. "That is the word of

a warrior who will have the female's thighs open wide and who will listen to her sweet cries of surrender as her wet pussy rides my cock for hours, draining me dry, taking my seed."

By the gods, that was *too much* fucking information. I had no response. I should have been able to cheer for Tane, but the tension in my shoulders and chest moved up into my throat and I couldn't force myself to speak or move. I could only watch and hate every male here for his ability to claim her. And Braun for his strategy to fucking *woo* her.

I shouldn't have come to the pits. Part of me knew watching this was a bad idea. No warrior would ever be worthy of her. Not one on this pathetic prison world. But neither could I bear the idea of *not* knowing who she would belong to, who would be charged with protecting her. She was an addiction I had been unable to best since her arrival a few weeks ago. My interest in her completely unwanted and impossible. My cock was ruling my mind. I'd had to take it in hand in the shower tube often enough to will it down, but no matter how many times I sought release, my body remained hard and aching. For her.

Leaning back, I crossed my arms and tried to look unaffected as I watched Tane's fist connect with the Prillon warrior's jaw, sending him reeling backward into the crowd along the fighting pit's edges. The shouting warriors seated there propped him up and shoved him back into the center of the pit where Tane delivered another powerful blow. So far, he was besting the Prillon warrior without calling on his beast. The young Prillon male was fighting a losing battle and he knew it, the swagger leaving his step and his shoulders slumping when another warrior, Tyran, stepped between the two combatants.

Tyran was a Prillon warrior and had a human female as his mate. Kristin. He shared her with his second, another warrior named Hunt. She was beautiful, and a warrior in her own right, like Gwen. I did not know how they could allow their female to work on missions hunting the Hive, but Kristin did so every day, part of a special group of warriors led by an Everian Hunter named Kiel.

Unlike the young Prillon fighting Tane, Tyran was rumored to be the strongest cyborg on the planet with implants running not just through parts of his body, but imbedded deeply in both muscle and bone. He was a legend in the pits but had stopped fighting once he was mated. It seemed he had other, more pleasant ways, to ease his anger and aggression.

I envied him the newfound method of release.

Tyran stepped into the center and proclaimed Tane the victor. Braun settled back, more relaxed now that Tyran had arrived. That warrior would not allow things to get too far out of hand, and he was strong enough to handle Tane, even if the Atlan went into beast mode.

"Told you Tane would win."

"It's not over yet," I reminded Braun.

"Yes, it is. He didn't even use his beast."

But he would. We both knew he would. "Stupid to challenge an Atlan," I added, referring to the young Prillon.

"Yes. None but Tyran, or perhaps the Hunter, could defeat one of us."

One of us. He included me among the Atlan ranks, as always, but I was not one of them. Never could be.

The next two fights went as expected until four warriors remained. Tane, two Prillon warriors, and a male from Trion whose skin shone silver in the afternoon light. I had not met him, but he was rumored to be more machine than man, and his fighting instincts were superb.

Tyran raised his hand, waiting for the crowd of warriors watching to quiet. "Here are the remaining four. Chance will decide their fates." Tyran held out a deck of cards, face down. "Highest values will fight first."

The crowd cheered again as the warriors each drew a card and lifted it into the air. The two Prillon warriors would face off against each other first. Then Tane would fight the male from Trion. After that, they would be down to two and the champion would be the last male standing.

Every single one of the four looked smug. Confident. As if Gwen already belonged to him. I wanted to jump into the pit and pummel them all into dust, but I didn't dare move, not even to frown. Stone. I must be like Stone.

A woman's bellow of rage filled the air and the cheering crowd of warriors went silent.

The door built into the side wall of the fighting ring was flung open, striking the side with a loud bang as Gwen marched into view wearing full battle armor. Her hair flowed down her back like black flames and fury rolled off her shoulders in almost perceptible waves. Eyes narrowed, muscles tense, she looked like a warrior goddess, too beautiful to be real. My breath caught, my cock lengthened at the sight of her.

Two other human women, both mated to Colony warriors, stood behind her in formation, like a strike squad, but they paled in comparison to Gwen's fire and I ignored them easily.

"What the hell do you think you're doing here?" Gwen yelled at Tane, clenching her fists. The giant Atlan Warlord actually flinched, as if he were a small boy being scolded by his mother.

Tane looked confused, then bowed before her. "My lady... I—"

"Don't you dare *my lady* me!" She marched up to his towering form, completely unafraid.

Next to me, Braun could barely contain his laughter, his shoulders shaking quietly as he watched the drama unfold. I wanted to punch him as well... for being right, for understanding more about Gwen than I had.

Covered in sweat and blood, the four warriors turned as one to face her, closing in, pleading their individual cases. I could not hear what they said, but none of it pleased her. Her hands moved to her hips, her head tilted to the side as if she listened and considered their words. But her eyes were like fire, feminine fury shining brightly. Fuck, she was gorgeous.

Braun's increasingly smug smile had my hands clenching into fists of my own as he leaned back and put his hands behind his head, stretching. Resting. Amused.

I looked back to Gwen, afraid if I kept my gaze on Braun I would punch that knowing and very possessive look right off his face. The males in the pit had lost any chance they had with her now. Braun just had to wait until she pulverized them all and then step in.

Gwen's gaze darted up into the stands and Braun held his breath as her attention flitted over him, then moved to me.

Air trapped in my lungs, her gaze like a physical blow, the gaze narrowing, her cheeks flushing even darker.

Yes, I wanted to be the one to put color in her cheeks. I

had to wonder how far down it crept beneath her armor, if her nipples were that same deep shade.

It was over in half a second. The glance. The look. The stare. The intensity.

Gwen looked away, rolling up the sleeves of her uniform shirt, although I had no idea why. Her voice, when she spoke, was not overly loud, but cold. Hard. "You want to fight? Okay. Let's roll."

Moving almost too fast to track, Gwen lifted the closest Prillon warrior and threw him even farther than Tane had thrown his opponent earlier. The Prillon offered no resistance, rolling to his feet after he landed, keeping his distance. When the other three warriors backed off with their hands out in front of them, clearly refusing to touch her, she kept pace, shoving the Trion warrior in the chest. She attacked in silence, each strike of her hands on male flesh loud in the distinct quiet. The warriors watching had no idea what to do. Cheer? Cringe?

The silence seemed to enrage her, for she yelled as much at the crowd as she did the four fools left in the fight. "Come on. Fuck all of you. You wanted to fight. Let's fight."

"Gwen, are you sure about this? I think we should wait for Maxim." Rachel, the governor's mate who stood near the open doorway, tried to plead with the irate female but to no avail.

"Get out of here, ladies." Gwen looked over her shoulder at the other two human females, motioning them away with a graceful wave of her hand. "This has nothing to do with you. These idiots should know *exactly* who they're messing with. Who they're fighting over like dogs would over a piece of meat."

Kristin, Tyran's mate, burst into laughter, taking hold of

his hand and leading him away when he would have interfered. Shocked, I watched the strongest male on the planet let the small human female—*his* human female—to pull him *away* from the fight. Braun had been right; Kristin believed herself independent, in control of her mate. He was *allowing* her to lead him away.

Looking back over her shoulder, Kristin had a huge, happy smile on her face. "Go get 'em, girlfriend."

Gwen smiled then, coldly. Darkly and full of menace. "Oh, I will. I'm going to kick ass and take names."

I had no idea why she needed the names of warriors already familiar to her, the Earth slang beyond me, but I had a feeling it wasn't anything good.

2

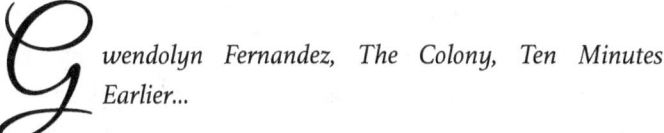

Gwendolyn Fernandez, The Colony, Ten Minutes Earlier...

THE HAMMER I swung was at least four feet long. The heavy, blunted end was designed to pulverize rock in the caves beneath The Colony's surface. Designed for an Atlan or a Prillon warrior, not a five-foot-five female from Earth.

Had I been normal—still fully human—I wouldn't have been able to lift it, let alone swing it in a wide arc and bring it crashing down on the wall in my friend, Kristin's, living room.

I'd been at it for over an hour, and barely broken a sweat, or worked the edge off my frustration. I was a hamster on a wheel on this stupid planet, and every oversized man-child here thought I not only needed a keeper, but wanted a big, bad alpha male to tell me what to do, what to eat, what to wear. Some Prillon had offered to put a *collar* around my neck so he could read my emotions or some shit.

The thought made me feel violated. The chaos of my mind was not a pretty place right now. I definitely didn't need to give a Prillon warrior—or two—access to the inner sanctum. What they'd find would probably scare them. Hell, most of the time the thoughts running through my mind scared *me*. Thus, me beating the shit out of Kristin's wall.

I swung the hammer again, harder, taking down a chunk twice my size with one blow. I didn't hear the door open, but it must have, because I was no longer alone.

"What the hell, Gwen? When I said I wanted the wall torn down to make this space bigger, I wasn't thinking right now, and I wasn't thinking you'd do it." Kristin's voice broke through the noise I made while smashing the wall to bits. I looked over my shoulder at my friend, the dust swirling around me like I was Pigpen from the *Charlie Brown* cartoon. Kristin wore the familiar body armor, as if she'd just come back from a mission, which she had.

"Don't worry. I closed the door to the baby's room so no dust would get in there." Kristin had a little one, a beautiful baby girl and two doting mates who treated her like a goddess.

But *she* was allowed to go on missions. To hunt for the Hive. Her mates had to be the *only* reasonable aliens on the whole damn planet.

And she wasn't even a cyborg. She was one-hundred-percent human. A volunteer. An Interstellar Bride sent from Earth when she'd been matched to her primary mate, Tyran, a tough as nails Prillon who had about the same amount of cyborg tech as I did. Tyran was strong. Super strong. One of only two warriors on the planet I wasn't sure I could best in a fight.

And he already had a mate. Kristin. My thoughts shifted away from him. Not that I'd go after a guy who was mated, but he definitely wasn't interested. He only had eyes for Kristin. And that was how it should be.

The other male on The Colony who melted my butter? Well, he was a loner. Quiet. Massive. Everyone I'd asked said he was an Atlan, but there was something different about him. Something that made my body clench with heat and my pussy ache with emptiness. Of all the males I'd met since being denied a return to Earth and basically left out here to rot, he was the only one who interested me in the slightest.

Makarios.

So, of course, he was one of the few who'd shown absolutely no interest in me. None. Not one stolen glance. No eye contact. Nada.

Big fat zero.

The only thing that saved my shattered ego was that he didn't seem to talk to anyone—male or female—except the two other Atlans he'd been with when the trio had escaped from the Hive. Braun, Tane and Makarios. The three Atlan Musketeers. All three of them were gorgeous, I had to admit it. But there was something about Makarios that put me on edge.

The others called him Mak, but when I looked at him, I pretty much just stopped thinking. Even his name was erotic. I wanted him. I wanted him to unleash some of that restrained control all over me. I didn't want forever, just long enough to scratch an itch or two. My sexual dry spell extended all the way back to Earth. Too long to go without a man-induced orgasm. Or two. Hell, with Mak, it would be at least three, I was sure.

It was well known that he didn't want a mate. The rumor-mill claimed he'd recently tried to escape The Colony—obviously, that hadn't worked—and that he wasn't even Coalition, but one who was cast out from Rogue 5. Maybe he was part Atlan and part whatever sexy beast roamed the Rogue 5 moon's home planet of Hyperion. All I'd ever heard about Rogue 5 was that they were a bunch of pirates and smugglers who belonged to very strict gangs. No loyalty to anyone but each other. The talk I'd heard said that originally, Mak had only been captured by the Hive because he was sitting in the brig of a Coalition ship when the Hive attacked. That he was nothing more than a Rogue 5 criminal with *really* bad luck. Wrong place, wrong time and he ended up with Hive integrations and a life stuck on The Colony.

But when I looked into his eyes, I didn't see a criminal. I saw a restlessness and rage I understood all too well. We were the same, me and Makarios. Trapped. Prisoners.

Freaks.

I swung the hammer. Harder.

The section of wall burst into a cloud of dust…

…and the ceiling splintered out in a web of hairline cracks above our heads.

"Holy shit, woman. That's enough!" Kristin closed the distance and took the hammer from me. I grinned when she was forced to drop it with a loud *oomph*. "How the hell did you even lift that thing?"

"Superfreak, remember?" I'd broken into her quarters to take care of the wall for her while she was out. Her idea to have it torn down one she'd shared in a late-night gab fest over a cup of Atlan wine, one of the few true pleasures to be found on this God-forsaken planet. And knowing she was off somewhere fighting while I resorted to breaking and entering to keep myself occupied somehow made the destruction less satisfying than I'd hoped. Still, it was better than going back down to the governor's office and arguing with him again. And a hell of a lot better than going down to the cafeteria and being eye-balled like the prize broodmare at a horse show.

"Stop saying that. If you were such a freak, every male on the base wouldn't be trying to get your attention."

"Couldn't have anything to do with the fact that I'm the only single female within light years of this place, could it? Last two people on a deserted island. Remember that game?"

Kristin laughed. "Oh, yeah. I always chose Detective Amaro."

I nearly choked, but coughed instead, waving at the cloud of dust settling around me to cover my reaction. "Seriously? From that crime show?" The detective was a very popular character on an Earth crime drama on TV. At least it had been when I left Earth. He was a badass who always got the bad guy. And I knew Kristin used to be FBI. But still. "Really? Why?"

Kristin's eyes closed and a dreamy expression came over her face. "His eyes were so intense. You know? And he had that uniform, and those handcuffs. The gun. He was just strong and sexy and—"

"Bossy and dominant and just like Tyran and Hunt."

Kristin opened her eyes, laughing now. "I guess so."

I tilted my head toward the bedroom. "Do I need to ask if all the bindings on the corners of that bed are for you or your mates?"

"I'll never tell." She looked back down at the mess on her floor but I couldn't miss the blush on her cheeks. There was no doubt she was well-satisfied by her mates, with or without restraints. "But I think you might need a little bit of attention from a special investigator of your own, if you know what I mean."

"Yeah, well, that's not going to happen." I pointed at the rubble on the floor. "You wanted this little remodeling done and I needed to work off some steam," I replied, inspecting what used to be a wall. The whole thing was broken to bits.

The sturdy wall hadn't stood a chance against my strength. My *cyborg* strength. The Hive had turned me into a certified bad-ass. The Bionic Woman. Whatever building material was used crumbled beneath the swing of the sledgehammer like a dried-up gingerbread house under the destructive glee of a toddler's foot. Yeah, being strong, like wicked strong, was a good thing. I didn't have to worry about some guy getting handsy—if I didn't want it—and I could completely take care of myself. At the same time, it was the reason I was so pissed off, taking out the wall between my friend's living room and dining room areas.

Kristin sneezed. "Steam? Let's call a spade a spade, sister. What you need isn't going to be found in here."

I frowned. "Yeah, well, it got you the big room you wanted." I pointed to the almost completely demolished wall.

"True." She nudged a larger piece of refuse with the toe of her boot. "I'm guessing you're not going to clean up the mess?" she asked, tapping her finger to her lips.

I laughed. "No way. I'm just the demo team. You've got two strong men who can haul away the debris."

She rolled her eyes, but she was grinning. "They are so not going to be happy about this."

I didn't care. I'd needed to break something, and she gave me the opportunity I needed to smash and destroy without getting in trouble with the governor.

Again.

"Look, I've been trying to mind my own business," she said in a rush.

"You have?"

"Yes, I have. But, seriously, what's the real reason for all this?" She waved her finger back and forth, pointing to the fifteen-foot-long pile of rubble. There was no judgment or expectation in her gaze, just pure curiosity. She was a woman. FBI. She was still a soldier, the armor she wore and weapon on her hip proof of that. If anyone would understand, it would be her. Not Rachel, the freakishly brilliant scientist, or Lindsey, the writer. There was one other woman from Earth I'd heard about and she didn't live on The Colony. A former instructor at the Coalition Academy had mated to an Atlan from The Colony, but they were now out in space working on some top-secret spy crap together. Out. In. Space. Not stuck, trapped on the exile planet.

And here I was, former-military, four-year member of a Coalition ReCon team, a demolitions expert, ungodly strong, Hive-enhanced, cyborg freak. I'd survived hell and came out the other side stronger. Faster.

Alone.

And the governor refused to let me leave the planet. Go on missions. Do *anything* fun. I felt like the Incredible Hulk with nothing to smash.

And these males trying to claim me? They didn't know me. I'd never even held a conversation with most of them. I hadn't been matched to them through the Interstellar Brides matching protocols. I was female. Available. *Breedable.*

Maybe. After what the Hive did to me, I didn't even know if I could still have children, let alone want to raise them here. And I hadn't bothered to ask the doctors at the med unit because getting a gyno exam in space after everything else I'd been through did *not* sound appealing.

Kristin continued to stare at me, waiting for an answer I was too proud to give her.

"I'm fine. Can't a friend do something nice for you?" I asked.

She gave me a look that screamed, *Girl, please.* "Nice would be making all the mess disappear before my men get back," she countered. "What gives, Gwen?"

"You know the answer," I grumbled, reaching for the sledgehammer's handle and leaning on the sturdy length.

Her eyebrows went up and waited.

"The men... they're weird around me. Annoying. Frustrating. And I can't go on any missions. The governor has grounded me until I'm mated. Which is ridiculous and a total double standard. I'm a prisoner. I can't fight. I can't fly. I can't go home. I'm losing my mind on this planet."

She remained quiet, letting me vent, even though I was dissing her new home, the place she'd been matched to through the Interstellar Brides Program. She'd *chosen* to come here, to *stay* here permanently. It was her life and she seemed happy. But I didn't belong here and the fact that the governor wouldn't allow me to go on missions, to at least get 'out there' was making me lose my mind. All the male attention didn't help, it just made me feel like more of a freak. I could have all the male company I wanted, and yet I was lonelier than I'd ever been in my life. The irony wasn't lost on me.

Kristin bit her lip and winced at my words. "Shit. I need

to tell you something. Please don't get mad. I was hoping it was a joke that would just blow over, but—"

"What?" I asked. I'd known her for a short time, but could read her easily, and I did *not* like the downcast eyes and pale face she was keeping averted.

"You're so not going to like this."

"What? Just spit it out." Dread coiled to settle in my gut like the dust around me.

"Captain Marz, the Prillon?"

"Yes." I knew him well enough. I'd had to turn him away from my door multiple times the last few weeks. He was all right. He tried. Brought me flowers, for heaven's sake—I suspected Rachel or Kristin had suggested that one. But there was no spark there. I looked at him and felt... nothing. "What about him?"

"He issued a tournament challenge. They're in the fighting pit right now deciding who gets to claim you."

Deciding who gets to claim you.

"Is this a joke? Because it's not funny."

She put her hand over her face as if afraid to look at me. Shook her head. "No. Eight warriors. Whoever wins gets to claim you. All of them have agreed to the terms. The rest of the warriors started a betting pool. The whole base had to either enter the challenge or agree to leave you alone. Tane, the Atlan, is getting two-to-one odds. He's the favorite to win."

"WHAT?" I roared. I picked up the sledgehammer and hit the last dangling bit of stone wall with more force than necessary. It not only broke free but flew into the other room and landed on Kristin's dining table, denting the metal surface. "The governor *agreed* to this?" I was going to kill that Prillon. I'd have to beg Rachel's forgiveness after I ended him, but this was too much.

"I don't think so—"

Good. I wouldn't have to kill him.

"—and Rachel and I just heard about it. She's on her way. She had to send someone to get Maxim. He's down in one of the mines and the comms are out. I went to your quarters first. When you weren't there, I came here."

"I can't believe this. It's barbaric." And hurtful. And wrong. How dare they presume to decide whom I would *belong to?* Whom I had to *have sex with?* And without even asking me? What was this? The 1500s?

The flowers didn't work, so Captain Marz decided to just challenge the whole rest of the base to a tournament with me as the prize? And who were the other idiots who'd agreed?

The whole base, apparently.

What if I decided I wanted someone else? A man from Earth? A Hunter, like Kiel. But a Prillon? No. The whole mind-meld, collar thing freaked me out. And two mates? Or three, as I'd heard the Vikens had started doing? Um, no. One man was enough for me. Especially if he was big and fierce and looked like Makarios.

Oh, shit. This was not happening. No. Fucking. Way. "They're fighting in the pits? Right now? This very second?"

"Come on. It's pretty hot, right, the strongest, sexiest men fighting over you?" Her hand moved up toward her neck and her fingertips stroked the green collar there—the outward indication she was matched to a Prillon—with a lustful look in her eyes. Her mates were incredible. I could not disagree. But they'd been matched. Chosen.

They hadn't forced themselves on her after beating up the other boys at the playground.

"No, it's not. I'm not a prize to be won. I am not *property*. No fucking way," I snarled. My poor mother would've been appalled at my language. But I was beyond caring. Somewhere between the little girl who used to play with dolls and bake cupcakes to make my daddy happy and now, I'd had the urge to please others disappear from my being. Maybe it was the cyborg parts. Maybe it was years of fighting a hard war, watching people die, caring too much. Somewhere in there, I'd lost the ability to put up with bullshit. And this was *way* above my tolerance level.

Kristin lifted her chin. "Then go do something about it." She looked around her living room, which I had definitely destroyed. "Go beat up some alien hotties before the ceiling falls on top of us. I'm begging you."

Wiping my hands together, I smiled. I was strong. Stronger than the men who were making me their prize. "Good idea."

I stomped past her, my stride long as I worked my way down the corridor and then outside. Distantly, I heard her on her comms unit as we went. "Rachel, get to the pits. Gwen needs another wingman." She followed me, which was fine. Since neither one of her mates was interested in me, they wouldn't be in the pits to suffer my wrath.

Wingman? It was a nice gesture, but it wasn't as if either Kristin or Rachel could back me up. No one could back me up. I was indestructible now that I'd spent some time with the Hive. Stronger than any almost any male on the planet. Faster than even the Everian Hunter, Kiel. They might think they were going to win me, but they were wrong. So fucking wrong. And if I had to smash some heads to prove it, I would. Once and for all.

Ten minutes later, I wasn't feeling any better. In fact, if I had the sledgehammer, I'd have smashed the stands surrounding the pit to rubble. "Why won't any of you fight me?" I shouted.

I was breathing hard, not because I was tired from tossing the males around the pit, but because I was pissed. So filled with fury I could barely see straight. My blood pressure was up, my heated lifeforce pumping through my body like the bass beat at a rave. But the cyborg part of me didn't feel a thing. My sight was perfect. My body buzzing with energy. It was my mind that was in turmoil, my heart that was breaking.

And I hadn't thought there were any pieces left big enough to break. I'd been wrong.

"We don't want to hurt you," one brave male said.

"We won't fight a female." That was Tane. The Atlan. Friend of Makarios. He seemed decent enough, but nothing was going to make up for the fact that I simply did not *want* him. I didn't want any of these overeager alpha males. The fact that they thought I was a prize to be won automatically eliminated them in my eyes.

If they'd been paying attention to a damn word I'd said the last few weeks, they would have known that.

But then, this wasn't about *me*. This was about *them*. Who's the biggest? The strongest? Who had muscles on muscles and the audacity to tell me who I had to give my body to?

I looked to Tane, narrowed my eyes. "Oh, you'll fight over me like a bunch of little boys with a new toy? You'll fuck me, mate me, but you won't fight me?" I'd die before I'd let one of them touch me now, and I was pretty sure that opinion was blazing from my eyes when I spoke to the Atlan. He shrunk away from me, as if I'd hurt him, then nodded, bowing at the waist.

Too late for that, big jerk.

"You are a very desirable female. We honor you with this battle for the right to court you."

It was unbelievable how different the customs were on the other planets. This wasn't Earth. I tried to use that knowledge to cool my rage. He thought they were being courteous, chivalrous. Respectful.

"I don't get any say then? No say in whether or not I can fight? Or whom I get to fuck? Or whom I mate? No choice at all? Because the winner of this"—I motioned with my finger pointed around the circle of four that remained standing —"is how you all treat your females? No choice. No desire. Not even dinner and a conversation? Straight to ownership of her body, and she doesn't have any say in the matter?" My voice was quiet, cold. I let the cyborg parts keep me calm and hoped I sounded more like a machine than the heart-broken romantic that was slowly bleeding to death inside. Now I wasn't just a freak who could never go home to Earth. Now I was just a piece of meat to be fought over.

"My lady—"

I spun about, looked to the male who'd called me that. "Don't call me—"

"Enough!" The governor's voice cut me off. Governor Maxim Rone walked with the air of a man used to being obeyed. Rachel was walking with him, nearly jogging to keep up with her mate's angry stride as he moved from the edge of the arena to the center. He was dressed in the loose clothing of someone who spent more time in meetings than in the field, the copper collar around his neck an exact match to the one Rachel wore. The connection between them all the more irritating to me at the moment. Maxim might sit at a desk, but he was still a Prillon warrior with years of battle experience. He was a force to be reckoned with, well-respected and elected to his post as the ruler of Base 3. The other males deferred to his judgment.

But I was not a male. And I did not belong on this planet.

I glared at Rachel.

"I only needed ten more minutes to finish them off."

She smiled, offered me a sheepish shrug. "I didn't want you to get hurt."

I rolled my eyes at that remote possibility but stayed quiet.

"The males showed you great respect in refusing to fight you." Unfortunately, Maxim's voice carried well because the other males seated around the arena stomped and clapped in agreement at his words. The governor crossed his arms and stared down at me. He was big, almost seven feet tall, his copper colored skin, dark hair and dark brown eyes reminded me of a Reese's Peanut Butter Cup. Of course, I would never tell him that. Or Rachel. And he wasn't exactly being candy-sweet at the moment either.

God, I missed chocolate.

"I'm stronger than they are. I'm a soldier, a member of the Coalition Fleet," I countered. "I've seen as much or more combat than every male here."

He gave a decisive nod. "You are all of those things, but

you are still female. We do not hurt females, not even in play. If you fight, you fight your enemies. We are not your enemies. You ask these males to dishonor themselves and their families when you ask them to fight you."

I huffed and glanced at Tane. The Atlan was beginning to look smug again, which added fuel to my fire. "That is such a double standard."

"It is no such thing. Coming from Earth, you are not as familiar with the ways of Atlan, Prillon and even Trion males. Other planets, too. Females are sacred. Respected. To hurt a female or a child is to betray everything we fought for, everything we continue to sacrifice to protect."

"Why am I the one in trouble here?" I waved my arm around as I spoke. "They're the ones who got it into their Neanderthal heads that the last one standing was going to claim me."

All of the men nodded, not the least bit contrite. Bloodied, sweaty and wearing torn clothing, they didn't deny their actions.

"The idea isn't a bad one."

"Are you fucking kidding me?" I shouted, completely aggravated. I tugged at my hair, paced in circles. I couldn't fight. What could I do? I was *trapped* on this planet. Caged like a wild animal.

"You're running wild here, Lieutenant."

"I'm not wild, Governor, I'm caged. Trapped." I walked until I stood nearly toe-to-toe with him and looked up, way up into his eyes. The resignation I saw there made my heart jolt with panic. He was going to do something here that I was *not* going to like. I could see it in that calm regret, hear it in the deep sigh that came rumbling out of his chest. "No. Not this. Just let me go on some missions. Let me go wild on a bunch of Hive instead of on these guys," I said, pointing at the four who had fought each other for me, but refused to fight *me*.

The governor slowly shook his head. "I cannot allow someone so close to losing control go on a mission. While I admit, these men taking it upon themselves to decide your fate was not the ideal solution, they aren't wrong. You need a mate."

"I'll fight to the death before I agree to this."

"And I'll put you in the brig until you calm down." He held up his fingers and nearly touched them to my lips when I drew another deep breath to argue. The shock of that almost touch made me pause as he continued. "It's not just you, but the males as well. They're practically feral over their desire to claim you. This base is starting to unravel, years of work and discipline are coming apart at the seams, and all because of one unmated female. The first and only mission I allowed you to take ended in disaster. Do you forget so easily?"

"No." I hadn't forgotten a single moment of that fiasco. Two Prillon warriors decided they were going to claim me while we were gone. The Atlan and two other Prillon warriors on the mission refused to allow them to approach me. A massive fight had broken out, the Atlan going into beast mode and destroying two small cruisers in the hangar before enough males arrived to break up the fight. And that had nothing to do with the actual fighting we'd been sent off to do. "Just order them to leave me alone."

"They are not human, Gwendolyn. You cannot expect them to behave as human men would on Earth. They are Coalition warriors, and they are losing control at the idea of you wandering the base unclaimed and unprotected. It goes against our very natures. I won't have it any longer. I can't." He added the last with some finality.

"So you're just going to let them fight over me? Winner take all?" I asked, stunned.

My stomach turned at the thought. While all four of the males before me were handsome, impressive male specimens, none were the one I would even consider. And *he* was in the stands. I'd locked eyes with Mak, the hot, brooding Atlan, when I caught a glimpse of him in the crowd. And one glimpse was enough to make my nipples go hard, my pussy clench with eager anticipation of being fucked. By him. Oh yes, he was all intense, alien. Hell, every one of them on The Colony was, but there was something about Mak that set him apart, that made me hot.

"Absolutely not," the governor said. "I have learned much from my mate." He turned to look at Rachel, who smiled and walked over to his side. He lifted his arm so she could slide in close to his side, then lowered it to rest across her shoulders, his fingers idly caressing her. "You will choose a mate. There is not a male here who would deny you."

The crowd roared in approval of that one, and I felt like an insect under a magnifying glass. Every male eye in the crowd was now focused exclusively on me. Shouting at me. Enticing me with flexed muscles or intense gazes. Good god. The governor had just unleashed the Kraken.

"Fine. I'll choose my own mate." I nodded once, relieved. "Good. If there's nothing else, I'll be going."

As I took a step toward the door I'd flung open, he called out, "You will choose a mate *now*. Right now. Before you leave the pit."

I froze then spun on my heel. "Now?"

"Now," he repeated. "You need a mate, to be claimed and marked so that the rest of the males know whom you belong to—"

"*Whom I belong to?*" I said, but he continued as if not hearing.

"—and will no longer find the need to fight in the mess hall, the outer courtyard or here in the pits."

"Are you serious?"

He gave one decisive nod. "Very. Choose a mate or one will be chosen for you."

"That's right. You will do as the governor says. Maybe then you'll be too busy to completely destroy our personal quarters," Tyran cut in, now standing beside Kristin. She rolled her eyes at her mate and then winked at me.

"Now," the governor said again, exerting his authority and using the example of my destruction of someone's living space as another reason for his haste. He raised his hand to silence the crowd and the volume went from melee to library in a matter of seconds, every male there watching me with hope in his eyes.

I glanced quickly into the stands. Found Makarios. Looked away.

Every male but *one*.

Damn. Makarios was scowling, his arms crossed over his chest, his face an unreadable slab of stone. He could have been watching paint dry. "But—"

"If you are mated, then you will no longer be a source of such disruption. You will be put back on active duty and allowed to go on missions," he added.

I bit my lip at that statement. At the fucking dangling carrot.

I angled my head down, stared at him through my

lashes. Okay, I'd bite. "Let me repeat that just so we're clear. I find myself a mate and I can go on missions again, even to fight the Hive."

"That's correct."

He wouldn't have tossed it out there if it weren't true. He was the governor, for Pete's sake. And, he'd said it in front of lots of people. Witnesses. He couldn't back out now.

I couldn't stay here on The Colony, grounded, for another day. The opportunity was too great. I just needed a mate. What did it matter? We could fuck and have fun and then I could go off on missions. Do my own thing. No connection except a good time. Any one of these males would be good in bed. But there was one who made me eager to get there. And now.

Even better, it was well known that he didn't want a mate at all. I did *not* need an overly protective, possessive alpha male bossing me around, thinking I *belonged* to him. I needed freedom, and a smoking hot tumble in the sheets.

Refusing to glance up into the stands, I focused my thoughts on the one who made me hot, who could make my time between missions filled with orgasms. The idea... and the thought of Mak's hands on me, his cock in me, was making me burn up with lust.

His eyes, light and piercing, would hold mine as he thrust into me. His skin was tanned, his jaw strong. With hair a little too long to be considered military cut, he stood out from the others. Even in the standard Coalition uniform, he stood out in a crowd. Taller than the other Atlans, he was a silent, sulking giant and I wanted to get under his skin and find out what made him tick. What made him hot. What made him burn.

There was nothing about him that overtly confirmed the

rumor that he wasn't Coalition military, that he wasn't a fighter at all. But I believed the gossip. And those in the know said he was a rebel and smuggler from Rogue 5. That he broke laws as easily as he could crack skulls. That his code of honor and loyalty belonged to his Legion on that ruled part of the rebel moon above the planet Hyperion. That he was *different*. Unique. Alone in the galaxy. One of a kind.

Exactly like me.

I put my hands on my hips. Hot sex. No strings. We'd both get what we wanted. "Fine."

The governor arched a brow. "That easily? I should have given you an ultimatum days ago. This base wouldn't be in such turmoil."

I pursed my lips, not pleased he'd put all the blame for things being a little crazy on me. It wasn't my fault the males were acting like a bunch of cavemen.

"Fighters, you willingly fought in the pit for this female. Will you now agree to allow her to select a mate?"

The four males puffed up their chests, lifted their chins. They nodded and agreed readily, no doubt confident, each of them, that I would choose him.

"Who do you choose, Gwendolyn Fernandez of Earth? Your decision will not be questioned, your answer final. Please state the warrior's name and planet of origin, so there will be no confusion. Whom do you declare as your mate?"

This wasn't the way I wanted to find a guy, but the perks were too good to pass up. A big cock attached to a hot guy *and* my freedom? I'd be able to go on missions, get off this planet for a while. The governor was being generous. If I didn't agree, I had to assume he would take the choice away from me. I would be mated to someone within the hour, someone he would probably select. It was all down to whether I would choose my own destiny or allow the decision to be made for me.

The whole situation was unfair, but then, that was life on The Colony. Suckage and more suckage after that. The males here were even worse off than I was, if I was being perfectly honest. I had my pick of hundreds of sexy, virile, eager males. And they only had the hope that they'd be matched to an Interstellar Bride, and that was only if the system, the testing made a match. Hope for a bride... and me.

I looked at the four males before me, then up into the stands. At him. I lifted my hand and pointed, taking a deep breath to steady my nerves. I had no idea how this was going to go down, if he'd be pleased or appalled. If he was interested or would hate me for trapping him. But I knew two things. One, I wanted his body pounding into mine. I wanted to touch him. Smell him. I wanted skin to skin contact in a big way.

And two? If the rumors were true, and I believed they were, Mak didn't want a mate. He didn't want to be on this planet any more than I did. We were both trapped. Prisoners. We could have fun and use each other for our own ends.

Of all the males here, he was the only one who would give me what I really wanted... hot sex with no strings. Besides, if I had to choose, I was going to go for what my traitorous body *craved*. "I choose Makarios Kronos of Rogue 5."

No one spoke. All was silent in the pit and the stands around it. Slowly, he stood.

Our gazes met.

Held.

I forgot to breathe.

Around us, no one moved. No one made a sound as a single beat of my pulse pounded through my ears like a bass drum. One beat.

Two.

Then all hell broke loose.

3

Mak, The Colony, The Pits

WHAT THE FUCK?

Every Prillon warrior in the stands was climbing down out of their seats to position himself behind Captain Marz. If Marz chose to fight, things were going to get ugly.

The Trion male grinned, bowed to me, then to Gwen, and calmly walked out of the pits through the swinging doors Gwen had flung open earlier.

Our friend, Tane, looked up at me like I'd just shot him in the back with an ion blaster but didn't move. In fact, every Atlan in the stands was seated like an unmoving mountain, waiting to see what I would do. Waiting for the call to fight for my right to claim the female. There weren't many Atlans on The Colony. Most didn't survive the Hive's attempts to turn them into monsters. But there were at least a dozen in the arena, counting Braun, Tane and myself.

We could give the Prillons below a fierce fight if every Atlan here went into beast mode. It would be a bloody, sweaty melee. Atlan and Prillon alike, they were all hungry for a good fight. Poised like snakes, ready to strike. No one would die, but everyone would bleed. All over the black-haired temptress who had just chosen a monster as her mate. The other males here were far more honorable than I. More deserving. I didn't deny it. I was a smuggler by trade, a pirate by choice. I chose my battles and my loyalties. And I was not Coalition. I shouldn't even be here.

Fuck. What a mess.

"What the fuck, Mak?" Braun hissed, turning to look at me. "You?"

Everyone in the pits was staring at me now, but no one else said a word, waiting to see what I would do.

Braun's eyes were wide and his entire body tense. As if he were stunned by the lieutenant's answer.

Well, my friend could join the fucking club for that, because I doubted anyone was more stunned than me.

Gwen chose me.

Me.

ME.

Holy fuck.

My heart pounded and I questioned if I'd heard her correctly. But I had, because Braun had heard it, too. Everyone heard her call my name. Even the governor, who had a smug look on his face and his arms crossed as he watched me just like the rest of them. The bastard knew I couldn't say no. Wouldn't say no. She was offering me a miracle, and a way off this fucking planet. And the stares? I ignored all of them. I only had eyes for Gwen because she hadn't looked away from me since she'd called my name.

My name. For a split second, I felt... special. Wanted. Desired, based on the need I saw in her eyes. Beneath the bravado, the intensity in her gaze, I saw hunger. Raw, unfiltered lust. The need for something she wanted *me* to give her. Not the four males who'd been fighting for her. Not anyone else in the stands. Hells, not even Braun.

Me.

I was growling before I could restrain the impulse, my fangs dropping in my mouth, eager to mark her, fill her with my seed, make her mine forever. But that was the animal side of my nature. Basic instinct. I was more than a Hyperion monster. I was a male with a mind and a will forged of iron.

I could take her. Fuck her. And keep the gods damned poison of my bite away from her. I would not be weak. I would not give in to the urge to claim her.

In fact, I highly doubted she wanted to be claimed. Not permanently. I knew the only reason she agreed to the governor's terms was to get off this planet. To go on missions and feel useful. Important. *Valued.*

We were the same, her and I. I heard it in her voice when she argued with the governor, begging to be allowed off this rock, begging to fight the Hive. Go out into space. Get out of the cage.

I'd stood slowly when she'd called my name, holding her gaze. I watched her attention roam over every inch of me with blatant hunger. But the moment of surprised elation was over. Clarity fell like the sharpest sword. Why me? Why the fuck would she choose me? I was from Rogue 5 of all places. And half Forsian besides. I was the *last* male she should choose in this arena.

And perhaps that was exactly why she had chosen me.

Before her declaration, I'd believed only a handful of warriors on the planet knew of my true origin. I assumed they all thought I was an Atlan.

I'd been wrong. She knew I wasn't Atlan. Knew I was from Rogue 5.

What else did she know?

Did she know the truth about me? About my bite? Did she know I couldn't claim her as my own?

If she did, she wasn't a fool for choosing me, she was taking a calculated risk. None of the rest of the males on this planet would allow her the kind of freedom I suspected she needed. No. These simpletons would get their hands on her, their cocks inside her, and turn into possessive, overly-protective, controlling *mates*. They'd want to breed her and keep her locked safely in her cage. A gilded cage, to be sure, but a prison all the same.

I didn't want a mate. I wanted a good fuck and more freedom. It appeared that she desired the same. Which was fine with me. The way she'd tossed the warriors below around like toys, I imagined it would take all my cross-breed strength to truly tame her in bed.

My cock rose to the challenge.

Her gaze fell to take in the very large, very visible bulge in my pants. And when she only put her hands on her hips and narrowed her dark eyes, almost daring me to say no, I knew she didn't plan to change her mind. And that dare? It made my cock weep and my balls ache. She was the most defiant female I'd ever met, of any race, anywhere in the galaxy. It only made me want to toss her over my shoulder and carry her off, drop her on my bed and dominate her. Oh, she'd hate that, submitting, but I knew the fight would make her wet. Because one thing I *did* know about her was that she was passionate, uninhibited. Wild. I looked forward to allowing her to work out all that feminine angst on me. Riding my cock with the deliberateness she gave to everything she did. Using me to soothe whatever had her perpetually riled. Perhaps she just needed an orgasm or two.

Or five.

Oh, I'd give them to her. And more. I'd give her so many, so much pleasure, that she'd be a sweaty, sated mess. Her mind would be empty, her body satisfied. Replete. Finally soothed.

Slowly, I moved.

Braun shifted to allow me to pass, to work my way to the steps that led down to the dirt pit where she stood. Waiting.

As I went, fighters moved out of my way, making a path for me. Perhaps waiting to see if Gwen would lift me and toss me across the pit like she had the Prillon.

She could try. I kept my eyes on hers as I went. Yes, I wanted that fire. Loved that it was directed at me. But this wasn't a mating in the sense of claiming her as my own forever. No, I couldn't have what the governor had with his mate, Rachel. Or Tyran with Kristin. Impossible. My cock wanted to fuck her. To spend in her tight pussy. To mark her. And my Hyperion fangs? I felt the pressure in my gums as I forced them to ascend. The beast within needed to bite her neck and make her mine. Permanently.

But because I was Hyperion *and* Forsian, my cock and my fangs had to work together for the true claiming. *This was the secret, the truth no one knew.* Not even the doctors who'd treated me when I'd arrived here.

A bite and the Forsian mating cock together would kill her. Forsian women dreamed of the day they'd take their mate's enlarged cock with the mating head deep in her pussy. A Forsian cock was compared to a club on the home world, filling their females to the extreme. Once a female agreed to the official claiming, the average male would be hard, his cock swelling in eagerness to fill, fuck and mark with his seed.

But a Forsian cock changed more than most. It grew. And grew. The wide head flared and it caught inside, impossible to pull from a female's tight passage until the claiming was complete. The couple was joined, locked together until the inner Forsian was satisfied that the female was truly and completely his. It took hours of fucking for a Forsian male's balls to be emptied of all his seed, for the cock to finally be satiated, for the pleasure to recede enough for his body to return to normal size—which was still larger than other races—and able to withdraw. Historically, it ensured the female was so filled with seed that the chances of being bred the first time were high. An innate and biological way for the Forsian race to continue.

By the time the cock was finally withdrawn, the female was unquestionably well-pleasured. Delirious with bliss. Sometimes even driven unconscious. But there was no question of the claiming. No male in the galaxy could miss the scent and marks on a mated female, no matter the race. All would know that she belonged to someone, that her pussy was her mate's and his alone. She was ruined for all others by the pleasure she found riding the engorged mating head. Once claimed, a Forsian female never longed for another.

As I stepped down onto the packed dirt, I knew Gwen could handle a Forsian mating cock. It would be a pleasure to finally get her stretched open with mine, and that alone would be fine.

But I wasn't just Forsian. Fuck, no.

Having her pussy pummeled by my club-sized cock along with my Hyperion fangs embedded deep and ruthlessly in her shoulder would surely kill her. It happened again and again with my rare kind. The fact that there were so few of us left, all males, was proof. Something about our genetic line, the mixture of Hyperion and Forsian DNA, turned the Hyperion bite of pleasure into a rare and deadly poison.

Gwen would die if I bit her. It was one thing to fuck her unconscious. My male ego could handle that. But I would not fuck her to death. I couldn't survive that kind of mistake. And that was why I'd avoided all females, for their own protection.

But now, somehow, the one female I'd avoided with deliberate intention had chosen me. Destroyed any chance I had to keep to my plan. To save her from me. For while we could fuck non-stop, I could never truly claim her as mine.

"He wasn't a choice. It was to be one of us," the bold Prillon, Captain Marz, insisted. He crossed his arms over his broad chest and there were three dozen Prillon warriors fanned out behind him prepared to support his claim.

The threat caused Gwen to break my gaze and she glared at the Prillon. "I was told to choose a mate. The only rule was that I had to do it now."

"He's not shown you any interest at all," Tane added.

Gwen narrowed her eyes, crossed her arms over her chest, mimicking the Prillon. She was so much smaller, appearing tiny surrounded by the four males, but I didn't miss the way her breasts were lifted by her actions. Her clothing did nothing to disguise her female shape, the curves that had incited the constant fighting across Base 3 since she'd arrived.

Tane's words were true. I'd done everything in my power to appear disinterested. If that Atlan only knew the extent of my obsession with her, he'd be shocked. I'd avoided her to save her and for that reason alone.

Now she was mine. She'd chosen me, and that changed everything.

Standing at the base of the seating area, I bunched my legs and leaped across the arena, landing squarely in front of Captain Marz and his supporters with my knees bent and a growl rumbling from my chest.

The Prillon didn't budge, standing his ground as I stood to my full height and looked down my nose at his nearly seven-foot frame. He was big. Strong. A good fighter. But I would smash him into dust if he tried to interfere.

"She's mine."

"By the gods, Mak." Tane moved to stand beside me, two Atlan sized warriors ready to fight. I was grateful for his support, and the hush that settled over the arena as first Braun, then every Atlan present stood as well. They would fight to support my claim. If Captain Marz didn't stand down, things would get bloody, and quickly.

My new mate stepped up next to me. "I can take care of myself, Makarios."

I looked away from Captain Marz to look down at her upturned face. She should have been sweaty and dirty from fighting, from throwing the Prillon idiot around the arena. But her skin looked dry and soft, utterly kissable. *She* looked utterly kissable.

Moving slowly, I lifted my hand to the side of her face, cradling her, shocked to my bones by the erotic jolt of lust the small contact sent roaring through my system. When she allowed my hand to wrap around the side of her neck, I pushed my advantage, burying my fingers in her hair and pulling her to my chest. "I know how strong you are, Gwendolyn of Earth. I know you are a warrior in your own right, capable of destroying these fools. But you will not. This fight is my right as your chosen. I will make them bleed for you."

"God, that's sexy." Her grin was permission, the sparkle in her eye hinting that she just might enjoy watching the show.

"The lieutenant's decision has been made," the governor said from behind me, his voice more than loud enough to carry to the farthest seats in the stands. "I will not renege on the agreement and neither shall anyone here. Warriors, your honor demands you respect her choice. Captain Marz, do you wish to deny a female the right to refuse your claim?" He looked to the four males as he said the last. Finally, he looked to me.

Shamed, Captain Marz bowed his head, first to Gwen, then to me. "Mak, she is yours."

Gwen shook her head. "Oh no."

The Prillon males grumbled almost as one, perhaps pleased that she'd changed her mind, eager to fight the gathered Atlans after all.

"I don't belong to *him*," Gwen said, looking from Captain Marz to me. She wrapped her small hand around my wrist and leaned into my touch, her head tilted back to rest in my hand where I still held her as she stared directly into my eyes in pure feminine challenge. "*He* belongs to me. Get that through your thick skulls."

She was making a claim of her own, and gods save me, her need to make it known that I was hers made my fangs burst free. There was nothing I could do to bring them back under control. Right then and there, my viewpoint on having a mate changed. I wanted her. I even had to shift my cock in my pants with my need for her. I didn't give a shit if everyone saw my desire for her. This female was contrary, feisty and ridiculously independent. She didn't need anyone's protection and she'd proved that by the way she'd tossed the Prillon around as if he were a pebble, not a seven-foot giant. And I wanted all that energy, that fire, focused squarely on me.

Now. My cock agreed. The sooner it was deep inside her the better. I wanted her fingernails digging into my skin. I wanted her with a need I'd never felt before. I'd fuck her until we both passed out; I just couldn't bite her. Sex. Skin on skin. Her pussy wrapped tight around my hard cock. If that was all I could have, it would have to be enough. For both of us.

When a Prillon stepped forward to argue some more, I put my arm out, my hand slamming into his chest and knocking him back a few steps.

"Mine," I growled, fangs on display. That one word, that newfound possessiveness, sealed my fate, the Hyperion beast raging within had come to the surface, ready for battle. My fangs were fully extended and I bared them, hissing a warning at anyone stupid enough to challenge me now, half out of my mind with the need to protect my female.

"Fuck, Mak." Even Tane backed away from me, his hands open, palms out in front of his chest as he walked backward. Slowly. "Listen, Mak. You in there? No one wants to take her from you. Got it?"

Gwen from Earth was mine. I wouldn't tell her that or she might rip my balls off and wear them for earrings, but she was. And I'd gladly be hers. I'd fuck her, get to see all that energy focused on the best way to get us both off. And often.

The governor stepped between me and the Prillon, breaking my beast's eye contact with the challenger, the threat to my female. "Enough, Mak. Get it under control and get your mate out of here."

When both Captain Marz and the governor backed off, I turned my head to my mate and held out my hand for her to take. To accept whatever it was I could give her. Part of me wanted to throw her over my shoulder and run, but I fought for self-control. Even now—no, especially now—it had to be her choice. Removing my hand from her hair, I held out the opposite, palm up, and waited like a gods damned saint.

No one would force *my female* to do anything. Not me and absolutely not the Prillon governor or any of the other warriors on this planet. She was mine now. Mine.

My entire body shuddered when the soft skin of her palm slid over mine. Gently, so very gently, I closed my hand around hers and that alone had my fangs retreating.

"Yes?" My voice hadn't fully recovered, but she understood.

"Yes."

That was all I needed. I lifted her off the ground, cradling her to my chest and walked away from the arena.

4

wen

"Put me down." I could walk. I wasn't some helpless little girl who needed to be carried around, no matter how good it felt to let go and trust someone else who seemed to want to take care of me. But I took care of myself. The fact was, being so up close and personal to the sexiest man I'd ever laid eyes on was making it difficult to breathe. He smelled like heat and sex and wood and some alien spice that made my pussy clench and my breasts grow heavy. I'd never smelled anything like it. Like *him*. I couldn't think. Thank god I'd never gotten too close to him before now, close enough to *smell* him. I'd have been climbing him like a monkey, ripping at his clothes.

I wasn't sure what to expect, but it wasn't for him to stop

moving completely and set me on my feet in the hallway that led to the private quarters. "No?"

"What?" I swayed, leaning toward him, drawing his scent deep into my body. We were alone and he knew I wanted him. Hell, I picked him out of every guy on the planet. I didn't have to pretend not to want him anymore.

"Mine?"

What was he asking me?

He moved to lift me into his arms again and I shoved his hands away.

"No?"

One word. Again. His voice was unnaturally deep and the fangs I could see peeking out from his upper lip were making me hot. I'd heard about the Hyperion bite, the rush of pleasure the women experienced when the males bit their mate, claimed them. I'd heard rumors that the bite was orgasmic, that black market dealers had created a synthesized version of the chemical and sold it from the shadows all over the galaxy. But I wouldn't have to track down a drug dealer out on a space station or back alley world. I had the real thing staring at me, asking me something. I wanted his cock inside me, his fangs deep. Which was stupid, because if he bit me, he'd never let me go. He'd be just as ridiculous and possessive as the rest of the cavemen on this planet.

I was just horny. Really, really horny. I didn't need fangs and serious stuff. I just needed to come and come hard. Surely this beast of a man could give me a few without any biting or... claiming stuff. It wasn't like he was a virgin. No fucking way had he been celibate his whole life. There was fucking and then there was claiming. I was fine with fucking. *Very* fine with just that.

"No?"

"What?"

But then again, he hadn't shown any interest in me before—other than the blatant bulge of his huge cock in his pants as he'd made his way down to me from the stands. *That* had been impossible to miss and that didn't mean claiming. It meant he obviously wanted to fuck, too.

It was biological. All of it. Why would I even think he'd *want* to bite me and make this permanent? That was foolish. It wasn't as if we'd been tested and matched like Rachel or Kristin and their mates through the Brides Program. We didn't know anything about each other. We could be hot for each other and still not get along. Sure, the look in his eyes in the fighting pit had been all male, and he'd been ready to fight every single Prillon there to win me, but that was *after* I chose him. At that point, it was probably more a matter of his male ego, of pride, than actual desire for me. It wasn't as if that pride would allow him to deny me in front of everyone.

I tried not to allow that thought to worm its way into my heart and make it hurt any more than the day's events had already caused, but I failed. Miserably. I was a freak with a pussy. The only available va-jay-jay on the planet and Mak wanted some. I wasn't super-model beautiful or cute, small and thin. I was a mixed-race mutt from Earth with cyborg parts and no feminine grace to speak of. I'd rather kill something than cook dinner for it. And now, in a moment of selfishness and weakness, I'd chosen a male who didn't even want me to begin with. I should have chosen Marz. Or Tane. Any of them. It wouldn't have made any difference because each and every one of them wanted to gobble me up with a spoon. But no, I had to trap the one male on the planet who didn't want anything to do with me in the first place.

First rate fuck up. I didn't think with my pussy very often, and this was why. Nothing but trouble, that needy bitch. "I'm sorry, Mak. I shouldn't have forced you."

"Gwen." He backed me up against the wall, and I used the cold, hard surface to brace myself as he got closer, his lips hovering over mine. "We have been talking in circles. Let me ask you plain. Yes or no, female? I want you. I want to fuck you, fill you with my seed. Devour you. Eat your pussy and make you scream my name. Yes or no? No more games."

Oh. Yes or no. He meant him. Him and me.

He wanted me after all. At least the fucking part. And I was a go for the screaming. Screaming meant orgasms. Lots of orgasms.

Mak didn't touch me, his entire being inches from mine, as if he were waiting for the answer to make contact. The heat from his frame was melting me where I stood, making my knees weak. Feeling bold, and desperate to touch him again, I lifted my arms and wrapped them around his neck, pulling his head down. He allowed me to move him and I took advantage, closing the distance between our lips. "Yes. And I'll speak plainly in return. I want you to fuck me."

My lips brushed his and I sighed, melting, pressing my body to his heat. His strength. God, he was huge. And strong. Maybe even stronger than me. I wouldn't have to hold back, worry about hurting him, breaking him. *Scaring him away.*

I tilted my head to the side almost instinctively. I wanted him to bite me. It was stupid, I knew, but right now, I didn't care. I wanted him to lose control, to really want me. Me. And not in a fuck and forget it way, despite what my head was screaming at me as I tilted my head even farther to the side, practically begging for his teeth. His mark. His *claim.*

I wanted to be more than a walking vagina, an available female. As stupid and empty a dream as it was with all the cyborg enhanced parts in my body, I wanted to feel beautiful and feminine and desired. My heart was in charge, swirling in Mak's scent and heat and alpha-male hotness. I wasn't thinking clearly. I'd regret it tomorrow, but my mind had been kicked to the backseat and my body was fully in charge. I knew it.

I didn't care.

"Bite me, Mak. Do it. I need you inside me."

With a groan that made my pussy clench with demand, Mak bent over me, nuzzling the exposed skin of my neck with his fangs. I shivered, the air frozen in my lungs in anticipation. Lust. One bite and I'd come, could feel the rage of need building in my body like a coiled spring pushed to the breaking point.

"No." It wasn't a question this time, but a refusal, and I stilled. Frowned. My fragile heart, which had just begun to beat again, slipped away, back into the dark corner where I'd left her all those weeks ago when the Hive took me. Broke me.

I'd put myself back together, stronger than before. Then Earth had rejected me. The males on this planet didn't know me, didn't bother to know me. They only wanted a female, a hot, wet pussy, someone to breed, and I was the only female available.

I was an idiot. I never should have agreed to the governor's stupid demand that I choose a mate. I should have chosen Tane, or even Captain Marz. At least they actually wanted to be with me. If I had to fuck someone, I didn't want to be with a male who didn't actually want me. A mating? That was a whole different level. I knew that. But when every other male in that arena would have had me naked and stuffed full of his cock already, Mak's refusal to bite me made me feel three times as stupid for following my little cracked heart. For choosing him.

For daring to hope. But then, I was nothing if not stubborn. It was how I'd survived this long.

I should have chosen the sure thing. I saw that now. Not this wild-card, Rogue 5 rebel, or smuggler. Criminal. Whatever. He was hot. I should have chosen with my head and not my raging hormones. "No?" I pushed against his chest. "You're right. This isn't going to work. I'm sorry."

"I will not." He pressed his body to mine, his rock-hard length obvious where it pressed into my belly. I squirmed as his scent washed over me. Through me. Got inside my head and made me forget what the fuck we were talking about.

Fucking. Mating. Sex. Hot, wet, messy, sweaty sex.

"Makarios." His name was a plea for mercy from my lips. It was all I had at the moment.

"I want you, Gwendolyn. I want to fill you with my cock. Give you pleasure." His lips closed on mine until they brushed against me with every heated word.

"Yes." *Yes. Yes. Yes.* That was what I wanted, too. "But you said no. Why are you kissing me if you don't want me?"

"Oh, I want you. We both agree to fucking, but I cannot bite you, Gwen. It is not possible. Do not ask it of me." Mak pulled his lips from mine and stared down into my eyes. I saw something there that made my heart skip a beat. Regret? Hurt? It was gone in an instant, but I couldn't forget it, vowed to discover the why behind his pain.

Thank god for stubborn pride, because it was the only thing capable of saving me at the moment. So, he didn't want to bite me. I mentally shrugged. Fine. I was obviously not his first choice for a mate. Fine. I'd been a fool for expecting more. For wanting more. A silly little girl with silly little dreams. And I'd thought the Hive had tortured them all out of me.

Surprise.

"Okay. You don't want to bite me. Whatever. But we both want to get off this planet. We can help each other, Mak. But my body needs..." My voice trailed off as his gaze darkened even further, the animalistic lust I saw there feeding my hunger once more. My heart still ached, but I told her to grow the fuck up, put on her big girl panties and deal. I was *not* walking away from multiple orgasms with the most virile, sexy, beast of a male I'd ever met. One who smelled like my every dark fantasy come to life.

"I will take care of you, female. You will scream my name so many times all other words will be forgotten." His gaze burned into mine. "You did not want a mate, Gwendolyn of Earth. I have not been tested by the Brides Program for the same reason. I respect your choice of me as your mate, even as the others here have not. We will both get what our bodies need, and then we will both be free."

"Free?"

"You heard the governor. Your bargain with him. You choose a mate and you can go on missions again. You chose me and now he will allow you to go fight once more."

"But I have to be... marked or whatever." I waved my hand between us.

He smiled... actually smiled. "Do not worry. Before this night is through, you will be well and truly marked. No male on this planet—or any other—will question that you belong to me."

I *hated* that term. *Belong to me.* As if. But, if it got me, like he said, back on missions, then I'd grit my teeth every time I heard those alpha male words.

I studied him. "And you? There has to be more to this than just wanting to get laid."

"I assume that term means fucking."

I nodded, remembering not everything translated with the NPUs in our brains.

"I wish to get off this planet as much as you. I need to be free. And I won't return."

I frowned. "Ever?"

His eyes narrowed and I saw the seriousness there. He was still aroused, but a deep need greater than getting off appeared.

"Ever."

I'd forced him into this. He was hot as hell and ready to fuck. I should be thrilled. A no-strings-attached kind of deal. One night and then we'd both get what we wanted.

I just had to wonder, when it came to fucking Mak, would one night be enough?

5

 wen

"All right. One night. We get naked, you mark me or whatever to make the governor happy. But as soon as you leave, I'll be right back to square one. The other unmated males won't back off."

Mak growled and anger flared in his eyes at my mention of other guys. Such a caveman.

"They will not touch you, Gwen. Ever. Unless I am dead."

The thought of him dead sobered me instantly. "What? What are you talking about?"

His expression was grim, and I believed every word. "A mate is sacred. So long as I live, no other will touch you. You do this, you'll be marked forever."

"No casual sex? No hook-ups?" Well, the thought of

being celibate the rest of my life really, really sucked, but so did being stuck on this damn planet forever. God, this sucked. But what choice did I have? I'd deal with the whole celibacy thing later. Much later.

"Where will you go?" That was *not* hurt in my voice. Absolutely not.

"I roam, Gwen. I will take a ship and go where the gods take me."

"Alone?"

"Unless you wish to run away with me. I will steal a vessel large enough for both of us and you can join me."

The idea made my heart leap, for all of a few seconds. Then the bitch came slamming right back down to reality. "I can't leave. There's too much to do, Mak."

His grin was full of regret, but I saw a hint of admiration in his eyes. "Too many Hive to kill?"

"Yes." He understood. At least that much. I couldn't leave the war knowing Earth was defenseless. That my old ReCon team was out there somewhere fighting and suffering. Dying. That the bastard who'd done this to me, *modified* my body to be his breeding machine, was still out there. "I don't run, Mak. I'm not a pirate or a smuggler. I fight. It's what I do."

His hips pressed forward, his hard cock pinning me to the wall, making me burn. "Even if you get burned, Gwen? Even if you die?"

"Even if I die."

He kissed me, hard. So hard I forgot to breathe. I clung to him until my lungs burned and my body screamed for oxygen, until my head swam with want. Then I pulled back. Let him go. It was hard. And I knew after this night together, letting go would be even more difficult tomorrow.

"All right, Mak. One night. No bite. No official mating. Then I get to go on fighting for the Coalition, and I'll help you get off this planet with a decent ship. Deal?"

I held out my hand between us to shake. He stared down at it, clearly not familiar with the Earth custom.

With a gasp of surprise, he lifted me into his arms again, almost jogging now as he carried me to his quarters. This time, I didn't protest. I held on tight and wished he would hurry, relief coursing through me. He wanted me, and he was in a hurry to have me. Oh, and the thick, hard cock pressing against my hip was perfect validation.

And since it was one night, I was glad he was hurrying.

When the door opened to his rooms, I looked around with a quick glance. The entire space was steel gray with splashes of a dark, burnished gold. Like evaporated sunshine left behind to glow forever. The pillows on the couch. Stripes on the bedding. One section of wall was the same color, a large, black symbol painted into the middle in a strange language I'd never seen before. He had a table with one chair, which struck me as both odd and sad. Most warriors had two, even though they weren't mated.

Guess Mak didn't get many visitors. Or didn't want any. Or have any intention of staying.

I looked at the huge bed as he carried me to it and tossed me down on my back. I bounced against the soft mattress. He loomed over me, his chest heaving, not from exertion but fighting for control. I'd imagined this moment, but I'd been limited to envisioning Mak in my quarters, his body half covered by my blood-orange sheets. That fantasy had worked to get me off all the nights I'd been alone, naked and in bed, my hand working between my thighs.

But those imaginings were nothing like the real thing.

And he was fully clothed. I didn't care where we were now, as long as it had a door, and privacy and we could get naked. Now.

And I would bet a thousand dollars that if I rolled over and buried my nose in his bed, the sheets would smell like him.

He watched me, seemingly gathering himself. But I didn't want him in control. I wasn't going to break. I wasn't exactly human. At least, not anymore.

No. I wanted him wild. I wanted him to feel like I did. I wanted fast and hard and rough.

Reaching down, I pulled my uniform shirt off in one quick movement, baring myself from the waist up. My dark hair fell in waves halfway down my back and I pulled my hair forward, teasing him.

His gaze roved and then he lunged.

With a laugh, I rolled out from under him at the last moment and jumped on top of him, straddling his hips, tearing at his shirt. I ripped the fabric down the center of his chest with a moan of pleasure as his hard length pressed against my clit through my uniform pants. I rode him, rubbing against him like a cat as I lowered my mouth to his exposed skin, tasting him. Smelling him. God, he was hot. I sucked one hard nipple into my mouth as his massive hands lifted to cup my bare breasts, pluck at my nipples. Yup, bare. I wasn't overly large in the boob department and I didn't like wearing a bra. I didn't need one, especially since the built-in armor worked well to disguise the whole nipple/headlight thing. My pussy flooded with wet heat and I arched into his hands, demanding more, never more thankful for going braless in my life.

"God, yes," I moaned.

I hadn't been with a man in years. Hadn't been with an alien... ever. And it was as if my body had stored up all that need, all that fire in a pressure cooker just waiting to explode. I needed this. I needed him. Bad.

I bit at Mak's chest, not hard enough to break the skin, but a challenge. A dare.

He answered with a rough growl.

I flew through space, unable to orient myself until I was flipped onto my back with Mak on top of me, between my legs. His cock pressed me into the bed, hard. I arched my hips and wrapped my legs around his thighs, needing more. I had no idea what came over me, but I was wild for him.

"Hurry. Please, please hurry," I gasped. Begged. For the first time in a while, I was panting, short of breath. "I want you inside me."

"No."

I narrowed my eyes at him. No? No? What the fuck, no? I *needed.*

Why did he keep saying that word, dammit? No other male on the planet would be such a pain in my ass like he was.

My control snapped and I lifted us both from the bed. I moved him until his back was against the wall, pressed to the dark symbol that I would investigate later. Much later. When my pussy didn't ache with emptiness. I pressed my hand to his chest, holding him in place as I tore his pants from his body with my free hand.

Boots. Fucking boots. He was still wearing boots. Whatever. That didn't matter because his cock was free. And it was huge. *Huge.* Magnificent.

Thick. Long. A deep plum color, a thick vein pulsed along the full length. The thick length I doubted I could close my fingers around when I gripped and stroked it. The crown was flared, broad, the slit at the center held a drop of pre-cum.

I licked my lips. That was for me and I was desperate to taste it. To feel how hard he was, how much he would stretch my mouth wide. No way could I deep throat that monster. My pussy ached to be opened up with that huge head, crammed full with every inch of him.

But first, I had to taste. God, did I. All other thought fled as I dropped to my knees and took the tip into my mouth. His scent intensified here, the heady and seductive combination unique to him making me almost dizzy. I moaned.

Would his cum taste like he smelled?

I sucked. Harder. Deeper. He groaned, was talking to me, but I didn't listen. I couldn't hear him through the pounding in my skull. I needed. I wanted to taste him. I wanted his cum in my mouth.

When I pulled back to take a breath, he moved too quickly for me to stop him. In the blink of an eye, our positions were reversed. *I* was pinned to the wall, his hand on my chest as he ripped my pants from my body with a fierceness I found incredibly arousing. I might be as strong as a superhero, but having a male show how powerful and virile he was—and with his raging cock out and glistening with my saliva—was such a turn on.

"Stay." The one word command made me tremble as he knelt and removed my boots. I stayed, because I wanted them off, too. Ridiculously, I liked his dominance.

He kicked his own boots off his feet and removed the rest of his uniform so that we both stood, completely naked. It was the first time anyone—besides the doctors at my arrival to The Colony—had seen my body after being captured by the Hive. I always ensured I was covered in long sleeves and pants to hide what those bastards had done. Everyone here had integrations, but this was my prick of vanity, of femininity, not allowing anyone to see them. I knew, if someone did, I might not be desirable.

I looked my fill of Mak, of what the Hive had done to him. A shoulder made of silver instead of his tanned flesh. A hip, thigh and knee of similar material. No wonder he was strong, fast. Powerful. When I lifted my gaze to his, he wasn't looking at me, at my eyes, but lower, roving over my body.

Immediately, I lifted my hands to cover myself. I hadn't been modest about the smaller size of my breasts or even the sight of my pussy. No, I covered one arm with the other, but it was no use. There were too many integrations all over my body to cover without a blanket.

I tried to shift, to turn to the side to hide as much of myself as I could, but his palm between my breasts kept me pinned.

"No. Do not attempt to hide what is mine from me, female."

"Mak... I, please," I begged, not exactly sure what to say.

Perhaps it was my tone that had his dark eyes meeting mine. Unfathomably dark and full of heat. Knowledge. Greed, somehow.

"I see you, Gwen."

I gave a rueful laugh. "Well, yeah. The lights are on."

Slowly, he shook his head.

"No, I see *you*. What you don't let anyone else see. Not just your body. I see your shame, your fear that you are not enough, perhaps that you are *too* much because of what the Hive did to you." He held me still as the silence stretched and his gaze roamed every part of me. Taking his time.

Nothing but acceptance—and lust—in his eyes. "You are beautiful. Perfect."

I huffed as I felt my cheeks heat, felt more exposed than I ever had in my life.

"Look at my cock. You might not believe my words but look at it. It's harder than it's ever been—"

"That's because it was in my mouth," I countered, but he ignored me and continued.

"—and that pre-cum dripping down the length, is all for you. *Look at it.*"

His growl had my chin tipping down, my gaze following the line of his body to his cock. Yeah, it was hard. So hard that it curved upward and actually brushed his navel. Pre-cum was seeping from the crown, the glistening fluid beading and sliding down the length to dampen the dark curls at the base.

"I see your breasts, your muscles, your silky hair, those plush lips. That gorgeous pussy. But I also see this."

He reached out and stroked my biceps, or what the Hive had done to my biceps, with the back of his fingers. I shouldn't have felt pleasure with that simple the touch, of course, since that part of me was all biosynthetic metal parts and integrations, but I *felt* it nonetheless. The Hive integrations were advanced, and the tissue there had become even more sensitive than normal flesh. His touch was like a flame, making me hot. Needy. I wanted more. I wanted him to touch me everywhere. Every single part of me wanted him. Human. Cyborg. Female.

"And this. No wonder you wish to go back to fighting those fuckers. You can use what they did against them."

His hand moved higher to my shoulder where the

silvery flesh matched his, then lower over my belly—thankfully unchanged—to my thigh. "All this power."

He dropped to his knees before me and stroked over my cyborg knee, calf and the top of my foot. He moved to the other foot and worked his way up until his fingers hovered over my pussy.

I held my breath.

"Not this," he said quietly, almost reverently. "No, this is all female."

He was wrong. There wasn't an inch of my body the Hive hadn't experimented on, hadn't adapted one way or another. But when he breathed deep, I flushed again, knowing he was picking up my arousal, the need for him that had slipped from me and coated the inside of my thighs. No way could he miss that either.

"All mine."

And then he lowered his head, licked up my seam in one long, slow slide.

I moaned, my fingers tangling in his hair, forgetting that I was all his for just tonight. Then we would both be free.

My thoughts fled until all I could think about was Mak and his wicked tongue on my clit. He moaned and the vibrations had me close to coming. Just. Like. That.

He took advantage of my distraction, standing and lifting me off the ground until my hips were shoulder height, all in one smooth motion. Being part cyborg seemed to have its advantages. "Put your legs over my shoulders," he commanded.

I did as he asked, pressing my back into the wall as I shifted, eager for what I knew was coming, his remembered words echoing in my mind like a broken record.

I want you. I want to fuck you, fill you with my seed. Devour you. Eat your pussy and make you scream my name.

Well, he'd had a sample of my pussy and if he'd stayed on his knees longer, I'd have definitely screamed his name. Held in place, back to the wall, I kept my right leg on his shoulder as he used his hand to push my left thigh wide, holding my left leg up, spreading me open for his inspection.

This position wouldn't have worked for mere mortals, but since we were both part cyborg, strong and powerful in a way the Hive intended, it was easy. And fucking hot.

The cool air hit the hot, swollen folds of my wet pussy and I arched my back with pleasure as he blew on my core, gently. Teasing me with what I knew he could do.

Fuck.

"Please. Do it. God, please."

He grinned as I buried my fingers in his hair once again, trying, without success, to force his mouth back to my pussy. He was immobile. I wrapped my hands around his head and pulled. Hard.

He was even stronger than I thought. He didn't budge. Not one inch. It was like I was trying to move a mountain. I couldn't get what I wanted. Couldn't best him from this position. I was at his mercy. Someone was stronger than me. Wouldn't give in to my demands. Yet I knew by that smile he was going to give me exactly what I wanted... but by his rules. And the thought made me so hot I felt the wet heat slip down to my ass and thighs.

"Mak. God. Please."

"That is third time you have begged me to touch you. It will not be the last."

I opened my mouth to argue but he slid two fingers deep

into my pussy, fingering me, spreading me open as his strong lips clamped down on my clit.

And I lost it. I was done for. That ruthless control I kept about myself? Gone. Torn to shreds by Mak. I'd actually begged. Pleaded. And he didn't laugh, didn't find me *less*. In fact, he liked it. Wanted it. He was right, he saw parts of me no one else saw. I was exposed, vulnerable and at his mercy, and not just because he had his face in my pussy.

The fact that he was about to make me come from just his fingers and mouth proved he had a control over me in a way I never imagined. And I never wanted it to stop.

6

Mak

I HAD a driving need to fuck Gwen. Hard. Bed-breaking, wall-smashing fucking. And we'd do it, too. My cock demanded it. My fangs... well, my fangs would be the only part of me that wouldn't be satisfied today. Or ever.

But *my* satisfaction wasn't my top priority. No. It was to get Gwen to scream, to feel her muscles tense, her thighs clamp down on my ears as I made her come. As I licked up every bit of her sweet, sticky essence. One whiff of her arousal for me, then one hit of it on my tongue had me ravenous.

The proof of her desire for me had my balls aching with the need to empty deep inside her. My cock swelled, and swelled. I recognized the change, the shift in my cock to mate, to fill, lock and remain deep in Gwen's pussy. It had never happened to me before, this possessive need to claim in the basest of ways. It was harder to stifle than my fangs, but somehow, I knew without the bite, the lock wouldn't happen. Oh, she'd take my massive cock for a ride, but I wouldn't remain deep within her. It wouldn't—couldn't—happen. My body wouldn't let it and neither would my mind.

Gwen might be mine to fuck, but not to keep. Especially since we'd just agreed to one night. She'd get my scent, get sent back on missions where she belonged and I'd get the fuck off The Colony.

Yet it was hard to think about tomorrow, about being in a different sector of the universe when she clawed at my hair, the way she succumbed so beautifully to the passion within her. She was stunning. I wanted to see it. To know I made her this way was heady. Fuck, it was thrilling. A sight to behold.

I knew she'd never given herself to another like this. She didn't behave like a virgin and I had no expectations of that, but this passionate nature of hers had just come out. For me and me alone. No one before me had seen her in such a state. No, she was balls-to-the-wall intense. Just as broody, as intense and fierce as I was. I saw it because I felt it in myself. Her need to escape, to escape even her own skin.

And right now, she wasn't thinking about anything. Not how she'd been forced to choose a mate, her need to go on missions, the fact that she was more than human now. The Hive. The Colony. Her role as lieutenant. Everything was gone from her mind, everything but me.

She could just be the female who submitted to my fingers, my mouth... and soon, once she came all over my face, my cock.

When I felt her muscles quiver, tasted the warm trickle

of her need on my tongue, felt her clit swell, I knew she was close. And when she arched her back, slammed her shoulders into the wall with the intensity of her orgasm, she was perfect.

Gwen. Lost to pleasure.

In that instant, while she practically ripped my hair out by the roots and screamed her release, I understood. Why the governor was obsessed with Rachel. Why Tyran and his second coveted Kristin. Why they would do anything for their mates. How they'd handed over their balls when their female arrived via transport from Earth, and were content in having done so.

Their possessiveness.

Their protectiveness.

Their need. Obsession. Desire. Affection. Mindless love.

No one else would see Gwen like this. Never. This... fire belonged to me. While I may have brought her to climax, she'd trusted me with herself, let go of any inhibitions, fears... everything. For me.

I knew that was a difficult thing for her, seemingly impossible being the only integrated Earth female on the planet. Hells, currently the only unmated female on the planet.

No longer. No. Fucking. Way.

This pussy, her slick, hot, pink flesh was mine. The tangy, sweet taste would linger only on my tongue. The scent of her would be all over my face, my chin, my cock. Every male who came near me would scent her, would know I'd taken what she'd offered so freely, even after I'd left.

If I'd known it would be like this, I'd have been among the fools trying to win her in that arena, just for this night alone. I'd have killed to possess her. Now I knew I would kill to protect her. And having my seed on her, marking her, would do just that long after I was gone.

When she was pressed, limp and sated, between me and the dented wall, her eyes flickered open.

"More," she growled, eyes wide and filled with heat.

I may have made her feel good, but she was far from done. *Far* from done. Not only would she carry my scent upon her, letting every male on the planet know who she belonged to, I would fill her pussy until she craved me. Needed me. Only me.

Lowering her to her feet, I pressed a hand against the wall, leaned in so we were eye to eye. Her cheeks were flushed the same shade of pink as her pussy. Her hair was a wild tangle and clung to her sweaty temples. Her breathing was ragged—something that didn't happen from tossing Prillons around the pit. She was... stunning.

"We are not done," I agreed.

With the back of my free hand, I wiped my mouth, then licked my lips. "I am marked. Your turn."

With her new quick reflexes, my cock was in her fist and she was pumping me before I blinked. My hips jerked involuntarily at the tight squeeze, the smooth slide. A groan ripped from my throat and I slapped my hand against the wall. Fuck. *Fuck!* It felt so good. So fucking good I gave myself over to it, to her. For just a few seconds, then I opened my eyes, looked at her.

Saw her looking down at my cock, at the way her hand was working me. With precision, ruthlessness. Intensity.

No. Shit. Fuck! "No," I snarled, and pulled my hips back, tugging my cock from her hold.

Her eyes flicked up to mine.

"What?" She licked her lips. "I know you're close, you swelled in my hand."

Any male would fucking swell in her hand if stroked with such talent.

"Holy crap, are you always this big?" she asked, her eyes were on my cock again. I glanced down between us, saw that it was bigger than it had ever been. Yeah, the mating instinct was making me grow and there was no way it would fit back in my pants.

"With you. Always," I replied. It was true. Until the true claiming was complete, my mate would know the pleasure of riding a Forsian cock. And when true claiming occurred, wouldn't be free from it until the biological need to fuck, to mate, to breed, was done. And that would take hours and an obscene amount of cum filling her pussy.

"You can get me off... this time," I added when she opened her mouth to speak. "Get my scent on you. Fuck, it will be hot to watch you smear it all over your body, to know that you're mine."

"I'm not—"

I pinned her with a dark stare.

"You're mine. As soon as you called out *my* name you became mine. Ask the governor. Ask anyone on the planet. Even the other females from Earth. You are mine, but I will honor your wishes. Our agreement. I will not bite you, force you into a mating you do not desire, but I *will* fuck you before this day is through. Hells, before this hour is through. I promise you, I will be hard and ready for you, over you and settled between those firm thighs. Sinking deep. Always hard."

Her gaze dropped to my cock and I felt a spurt of cum seep from the tip. I wasn't lying. The first stages of the mating cock had begun as soon as she called my name. It wouldn't go down all the way now until I claimed her. Perhaps if I thought of Hive torture it might diminish, but definitely not when she was in my presence. When I could smell her female scent. Her need. And once she was marked, when our scents were mingled... fuck. I just got harder.

"This first time can be with your hand, right here against the wall. But know this, Gwen, I will be balls deep in you soon enough."

Heat flared in her dark eyes and her gaze dropped to my cock. Leaning forward, she flicked her tongue over the tip. "You're giving me control?"

Was I? Would I stand still and allow her to work me to completion? If it felt like what she'd been doing, fuck yes. But after... when I got her beneath me? She'd know my dominance. "For now."

She shook her head.

"No?" I asked.

"If I get to be in control, then I don't want it this way."

I arched a brow, watched as the corner of her mouth turned up with a hint of challenge.

"Oh?"

Her hands pushed on my shoulders and I was launched backward and onto the bed. I bounced, but the bed frame collapsed beneath me, the mattress dropping a foot to the floor with a loud thump.

Naked and very pleased with herself, she stalked toward me. Nude and glorious. "If I'm in control, I'm taking that massive cock for a ride."

Fuck, yes.

"Grip the headboard."

I tilted my head down, gave her a stern look, but I completely forgot I didn't like being bossed around when she put one knee on the mattress and crawled toward me.

Naked.

Her small breasts were perfect swells beneath her, dark pink, hard-tipped nipples pointing toward the bed, her hair long down over her shoulders. Wide hips swayed with each foot she moved closer. A predator and I was her fucking prey.

Fuck yes. This worked for me.

Glancing up, I reached for the headboard, knew it would be in pieces before we were done. My fingers curled around the metal slats, gripped.

She worked her way up my body until she straddled me, her knees on either side of my hips. I was big, so big that she was spread wide, her pussy resting directly on my stomach. My cock brushed up along the seam of her ass and while I held on with a fucking death grip, my hips involuntarily bucked, spreading my pre-cum along that gorgeous ass, as if it knew it would soon get in there too, not just her pussy.

Her desire smeared all over my belly and I knew, while I was huge, her passage was well prepared for me.

"I can't believe I have you at my mercy," she whispered, studying me.

"Is that still what you think?" I countered.

Cocking her head to the side, she studied me. I watched the fall of her dark hair over her shoulder. "I think you're giving me control." She paused. "That as soon as I've had my turn, you'll have yours."

"I told you that you are mine. I will prove it before we leave this room."

"Don't you mean this bed?" she asked.

I lifted my hips, stroked my cock along her ass again. "You have a better imagination than that, I'm sure. We will not limit our fucking to a bed. I will give you what you need anytime. Any place."

She squirmed on top of me. "And what do you need?"

"Do you wish to talk while you have me pinned to the bed or do you wish to fuck?"

Her eyes widened, then narrowed just before she pushed up onto her knees, hovering over me. Sliding back so the broad crown of my cock was at her slick entrance, she met my gaze, held it as she slowly worked her way down onto me.

She gasped as my hard length began to stretch her open, as the head breached her. Lifting back up, she eased off, then pressed down. An inch, then retreated. Lower, but another inch, then back. She fucked herself slowly onto me.

"Jesus, Mak," she gasped, circling her hips, taking more and then more of me. "Do you ever end?"

It took a while for her to sit fully on my lap, to have my massive cock deep inside her. By then, my teeth were gritted, my molars dust. The metal of the headboard was bent from my grip and my control was close to snapping. I'd give her this. But only if she started to fucking move. My balls burned to fill her. My fangs ached to descend.

Every fiber of my being wanted her to move, to fuck herself on me. And when she did just that, placing her palms on my chest and lifting and lowering herself, I groaned. She was a sight to behold. The way she bit her lip and closed her eyes, giving over to the pleasure of me being inside her. Her breasts, while small, swayed slightly with her motions. Her waist was narrow, her hips wide. Her ass, fuck, I wanted to grip it in my hands and hang on. And the Hive integrations, the silvery hints of her new strength, only reminded me of how I could reduce her—once again—to the female within.

"I-I can't come like this. I need more."

I saw the frustration on her face mixed with her arousal.

"Touch yourself. That's it. Yes. Put those fingers on that hard, little gem and rub it. Show me what feels good. Ride my cock and get yourself off. I promise that when you do, your pussy's going to milk the cum right from my balls.

Maybe it was my dark words. Maybe it was the knowledge that I was right there with her, but she moved one hand down between us and she began to play. To circle and press as she began to fuck me faster, harder.

The combination had her inner walls clenching, squeezing me. The sound of her arousal was all I could hear over her ragged breathing.

"Mak!" she cried, coming all over me.

I did come then, her pussy milking the cum from me, just as I'd said. I couldn't hold it back. There was no chance. The pleasure was intense, the feel of her wet heat too much. She was just too perfect.

The slats of the headboard ripped away, and I had her flipped onto her back, my cock still deep inside her as we continued to come. I didn't let up, but fucked her hard, pushing us both into another orgasm.

Hells, I wasn't done. It wasn't the mating cock keeping me deep. It was this need, this obsession with Gwen. I needed it. I needed her.

"More," I growled, echoing her earlier words.

When her eyes flickered open, she smiled. Her hands slid down my sides and to my ass, pulled me closer—if that were possible.

"More," she repeated.

There would be no question, when we went to our mission meetings in the morning, that Gwen was marked and taken. Claiming her with my bite wasn't necessary.

When she clawed at my back, her body shuddering as another orgasm ripped through her, her pussy pulsing and rippling around my cock like a hot fist, the Hyperion beast awoke. I couldn't stop my fangs from descending, the urge to bite her so strong I buried them in the mattress as I pumped my seed into her yet again.

I wasn't sane in that moment. I knew it. But the beast within didn't care about rules or promises or honor. He simply *wanted*.

Gwen was mine. To fuck. To protect. To touch and pet and spoil. No one would fucking look at her if they wanted to keep breathing.

"Mak." Gwen's cry was sweet torment as she raised her hips beneath me, ankles locked behind my back, her incredible strength lifting us both up off the bed, driving my cock deep, demanding more.

I gave it to her. I gave her everything I could.

And the beast howled in pain. Denied his final claim. And with our agreement, denied anything more than right now. For this night would be it.

7

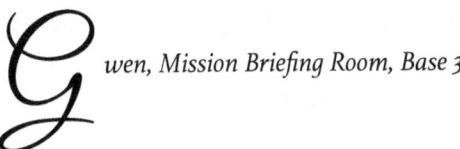

wen, Mission Briefing Room, Base 3

GOVERNOR RONE SAT in one of the large chairs that circled the round table and crossed his arms. He looked entirely too pleased with himself. Smug, even, for getting me mated. And to him that meant subdued. Under control.

Jerk.

But I couldn't exactly be mad at him either, not after the night I had. Mak sat next to me, his scent lingering on my skin, my pussy hot and aching and very, very hungry for more. I *was* a little subdued. Who wouldn't be after a wild night like ours?

Mak was an incredible lover. God, I'd lost track of the number of orgasms that he'd wrung from my body. And he hadn't freaked when I'd used my cyborg strength on him. At one point last night, I'd pressed him against the wall and taken him into my mouth until he came all over me, although I realized he wouldn't have put up any kind of fight. Not by the way he'd groaned and gripped my head in place until the last second when he pulled out and covered me. That man had so much cum in him, it was like he'd stored it up. We'd been in the bathing tube and I'd rubbed his essence all over my skin just to watch his eyes burn into me like they were doing now.

When the water washed it away he'd growled, fangs bared, lifted me from my knees and shoved my back against the wall, fucking me standing as the water cascaded down over both of us.

It had been erotic. The sexiest thing that ever happened to me. So far.

I wanted more. But I wasn't going to get it, and my pussy wasn't too excited about that. It hadn't ever been an issue before, but now being horny occupied my mind. Which was bad.

Mak's arm rested along the back of my chair. I should have protested, but since I was literally counting down the minutes until we'd leave on our mission and he'd leave me, I leaned into him instead, soaking up what I could get. I wasn't in love with him by any means, my heart not aching for him to stay. But my pussy? She was head-over-heels in lust and wanted more.

Tough sweetheart. You're not getting it. Get over it.

"The moon's atmosphere is highly toxic. Visibility is near zero, the air filled with a white acidic fog. You'll need to wear full space gear and be prepared for anything." The governor pointed to a small spot marked on the map of the moon we'd be targeting. A Hive transmission had been caught bouncing off the moon to the surface of The Colony.

Which meant the Hive had some kind of base, ship or communications center just over our heads.

The thought made my skin crawl because that meant they were focused on the planet. And if they were focused on the planet, that meant they might come here. Invade. Capture us. Again.

Captain Marz was the leader on this mission, and it was all I could do to look him in the eye after the whole pit fighting fuck-up the day before. But I did. In fact, I glared, not quite ready to forgive him yet. But I listened when he spoke because he wasn't rehashing it all, and so I wasn't going to either. And I'd follow him on a mission because, well, I wanted to go on a fucking mission, but also because I respected him as a fighter. I wouldn't let stupid alien mating rituals get in the way of our jobs.

"We'll be taking two ships, overlapping our scans. If one of us takes a hit or engages in battle, the other must take out the Hive communications before anything else. That is the first priority. Take down the fucking Hive comm."

"Understood." I couldn't wait to get up there and kick some Hive ass. I hoped Captain Marz and his Prillon friend, Vance, found the communications gear because I wanted to get down and dirty with some Hive assholes. Crush them. Maybe rip off an arm or two.

I should have been worn out from staying up half the night fucking, instead, I was energized.

"I will go with Lieutenant Fernandez." The Trion warrior seated next to the governor who spoke was not one I knew. But I didn't care. He was irrelevant. Mak and I had a plan, an agreement. He'd given me what I wanted, his scent all over me and more orgasms than I could count. Plus, I was here for the mission briefing, ready to go out and kick some Hive ass.

And true to their word, every male on The Colony I'd come across since we left Mak's quarters now treated me like I was no more or less interesting than any other member of the contaminated. They were honoring Mak's claim. I refused to think about how they could somehow, in their space alien way, scent his cum all over me—even though I'd washed it off.

As for our agreement? I'd keep to it, which meant it was time for me to pay up. I looked up at Mak, nodded for him to go ahead, that I was still in this with him.

A deal was a deal, no matter how much it sucked balls and made my hungry body want to weep. One night was not enough, and I had a feeling I was ruined for all other guys—not that they'd get near me now that I had Mak's scent all over me.

"I will accompany my mate," Mak said, giving the Trion fighter the Vulcan death stare. "I will keep her safe. I do not trust these weaklings to ensure her safety." Mak made the declaration with a cold, quiet voice that spoke more loudly than a shout would have.

The Trion looked to Governor Rone for guidance and kept his mouth shut, but I could see he was angry in every line in his body.

The governor leaned forward, his elbows on the table, hands clasped as he tilted his head, staring at both of us like a curious bloodhound sniffing out a lie. "I can scent your mating from here. Of that I have no doubt."

"Then what's the problem?" I asked, and I refused to think about the blush creeping into my cheeks at him sniffing out all the sex Mak and I'd had. "You said choose a mate. I chose Mak. Now you can deal with the consequences. If he is adamant about going with me, I will not sway him otherwise. You all wanted me to understand your customs, the way you're all so darn bossy, to go along with them." I shrugged. "I am. If he wants to go, then who am I to stop him?"

"You aren't," the governor said. "I'm the one to stop him."

The Prillon shook his head after the governor finished. "It's too soon for you to leave the planet, Makarios."

Mak rose to his full height and I sat back and grinned. God, he was magnificent. Truly.

"I don't give a shit what you think about me. Things have changed. She is mine!" His voice was a roar now, fangs fully extended as Mak pointed at me. Like there was any doubt who he was talking about. Two more guards rushed into the room at the outburst, but the governor raised his hand and they held back, waiting to see how this mess played out.

I was interested in seeing that myself. What I'd thought of as alien posturing before, I saw now as hot as fuck. At least with Mak all growly and alpha. I wanted to drag him out of the room and have my way with him.

"Calm down."

"She is mine," Mak repeated. "Mine! She does not go into battle without me. She is mine to protect. Mine." He was going full beast, or whatever alien version of it he possessed. I knew his fangs were down. Knew, from seeing him fight back the instinct to bite me last night that his eyes were probably glowing, that his muscles swelled, his fangs dripping with venom.

Leaning back, I put my feet up on the table, crossed my ankles and literally twiddled my thumbs. I wanted to laugh at the horrified expression on the governor's face. He soooo deserved this little Hyperion display of rage. I knew Mak was acting, but they didn't. All they knew was they could smell us on each other.

Such simple-minded males. As if that was the end of the discussion.

"Mak—" the governor began, but Mak was having none of it.

He leaned forward, put his hands on the table and glared at everyone around it. "I will kill anyone who tries to stop me. It is my right to protect her. I have no doubt if she'd chosen Marz or Tane they'd feel the same. And with Tane, you'd be dealing with an Atlan beast right now. Be thankful I'm only Hyperion and Forsian. *She. Is. Mine.*"

The governor sat back in his chair and ran a hand through his dark hair. I almost felt sorry for the guy. Almost.

"By the gods, I thought the Atlans were bad." The words were mumbled, then he sighed, motioning Mak to sit back down. "Fine. Marz and Vance will take the first section. You two will cover the second," he said, referring to me and Mak. "We don't know what we'll find, so this is recon only. If you have an open shot at destroying their comms, take it. Otherwise, note the location and return here so we can plan a full strike op. Got it? We're only going to get one chance at destroying it or the Hive will know we're on to them—and I don't want you to fuck it up."

"Yes, sir." I knew I looked like the Cheshire Cat about now. Knew, and didn't even try to hide the smug smile I felt tugging at the corners of my lips. We were going on a mission. Together. Our plan had worked. Mak and I, well, we were good at more than just fucking each other's brains out. I didn't have to look at him to know what he was thinking, feeling. And we could work this room like putty in a preschooler's hands. I hadn't felt this... connection to anyone in a long time. If ever.

"You leave in an hour. Head down to the hangar for flight checks." The governor's gaze met mine and I could have sworn I saw a glint of amusement there. "Earth females. I should have known you'd be trouble, even after picking a damned mate."

"The best kind of trouble." I hopped out of my chair, slapped Mak on the arm and tugged him along behind me. "Let's go, Mak. We've got a job to do."

Mak was on my heels. I could feel him hulking behind me like a storm cloud as we walked down the twisting corridors of Base 3. But it didn't bother me, it made me feel safe. Even if he'd been acting for the crowd in there so he could get sent on this mission—so he could leave me—even I'd believed he had some kind of primal urge to protect me. Just for a moment.

We'd accomplished our goal. I was heading out on a mission. My pussy no longer felt abandoned and neglected, I had the governor and all the males on the planet off my back and Makarios of Kronos was going home to Rogue 5.

Win-win. Just like we both wanted. So why did my feet grow heavier with every step toward the shuttle hangar? Toward good-bye.

God, this sucked. I didn't want a brooding, controlling, dominant Neanderthal for a mate. And yet, I wanted Mak. And he was all of those things. Every. Single. One.

I could hear him breathing, but he didn't speak. Didn't say a word. Didn't touch me. He was a shadow behind me and I wondered if he felt the same way. Were we both just shadows of our former selves? Not really living? Not really dying, either? Going through the motions until we got what we wanted—off this fucking planet?

And *that* was depressing as fuck because last night felt like living. I'd *felt* for the first time in a long, long while. Mak would head off to roam the galaxy like Han Solo and I'd return here, go on missions, but would I be able to feel again? My hand wouldn't give me the orgasms Mak could. And that was the kicker. I had exactly what I'd wanted. A life —while being on The Colony wasn't exactly home sweet home—with missions, with purpose once again.

Now I'd have that, thanks to Mak. Because since I chose him, he *wanted* me to go on missions, to do what I was supposed to do with my life. As long as my goal wasn't to be officially claimed by him, he was fine. He was leaving.

But somehow, over the course of one night, I wanted a tiny bit more. No, not tiny. Huge. I wanted Mak's huge cock. What hot-blooded female wouldn't? One taste—and I did mean *taste*—and I knew I'd ache for more. My pussy clenched at the thought of never being filled with his enormous cock.

Shaking my head to clear it, because I was being all girly and ridiculous, I stopped cold in the deserted hallway and turned around. "Thanks, Mak. That was perfect. You should win an Academy Award for that performance."

He stopped and frowned. "What is this award?"

I studied him. His fangs were still down. His skin flushed. His hands were in fists at his sides and his chest was heaving. What the hell? "It's an award given to actors back on Earth. What is wrong with you? Are you all right?" I reached up and placed my palm on his cheek. I couldn't reach his forehead, but I'd take what I could get.

He was hot to the touch. Burning up. "Are you sick? Do you guys get a fever?"

He lifted one hand and wrapped it gently around my wrist, holding my palm to his skin. "I was not acting, female."

It was my turn to frown. He hadn't been acting? "What? But everything went according to plan. You're going with me to the moon. We'll destroy the Hive up there and then you can go back to roaming the galaxy or whatever it was you'd been up to. Rogue 5, Forsia. Wherever it is you want to hang your hat." I used my thumb to pet him, because I could, and because standing so close to him made me want stupid things. Like to be more. But more what? Normal? Beautiful? Helpless? Perfect?

I didn't know what Mak wanted in a woman. But apparently, even after several rounds of fucking, I wasn't it. If I had been, those fangs would have been buried deep last night and I would have been screaming in pleasure as he made me his forever. Because the way Rachel and Kristin had said, their men had looked at each of them and wanted to claim them on the spot. There wasn't any of this one night stand stuff. It was forever with them.

But not Mak. It had been a trade. A bargain, with hot sex thrown in.

And as for claiming? God, I would have let him. I knew the truth. Couldn't lie to myself about my newfound weakness when it came to him. He was like a drug. I was hooked. What was wrong with me? Was there some kind of Forsian brainwash? Did his cock have magical powers? Something with his cum like I'd heard the Vikens had? Seed power?

I yanked my hand away, disgusted with myself. I was not

the kind of woman who trapped a damn man. Not my game. Never had been, never would be. Mak wanted to fuck and he wanted to leave The Colony. He'd been honest with me from the start. Being upset about it now was beneath me, especially since that was what I'd wanted, too. Me on missions. But that had been yesterday. "Let's get you home, Mak. You don't belong here any more than I do."

"Is this how you say good-bye, female?"

I frowned. "What do you mean?"

He looked over his shoulder at someone who passed by us in the hallway, but Mak was too big for me to see who it was. Gently, he cupped my biceps and led me into a briefing room, let the door slide closed behind us. It was identical to the one we'd just left, except this one was empty. His hand slapped against the wall, pressing the lock.

"We have an hour. What do you usually do before a mission?"

"Talk with my teammates."

His eyes drifted to my lips. "I have much better uses for your mouth than talking."

Oh.

Oh.

Holy. Fucking. Oh.

He dropped his hand and I stepped back. While I liked sucking his cock, I couldn't get much more in my mouth than that flared crown. And I'd tried. I undid the clasp on my pants, let them hang loose on my hips as I turned about and bent over the large table. Settling on my forearms, I glanced over my shoulder in invitation.

Mak watched my every move and his gaze settled on my upturned ass.

Between one second and the next, he was behind me.

Fingers tugged at the top of my pants and yanked them down so my ass was bare.

I expected him to tug open his own pants and fuck me. Instead, he spanked me.

I startled, felt the sting as it spread through my body. Pushing off, I spun around to face him. Big mistake. He was huge, hot, sexy and smelled like heaven. Instead of arguing, I wanted to touch. Sheesh. Pathetic. Still, I worked up the willpower to protest the heat spreading on my bottom.

"What the hell was that for?"

"Your mind wandered, worried," he said, cupping his cock that now stretched his mission pants to capacity. "Now you are here, with me. And while taking you from behind appeases the Hyperion in me, the Forsian is angry."

He opened his pants. Finally. Pulled out his cock, stroked it once.

Stepping into me, the backs of my thighs pressed into the hard table. I had nowhere to go.

"You have too many personalities to keep up with. Just tell me what you want."

"And you'll give it to me?"

I licked my lips, realizing the answer was yes. I'd give him whatever he wanted. After the previous night, I knew he might get what he wanted, but he'd give me what I needed. "That's my job as your mate."

For only a little while longer. So I'd take it. This last hour.

"A Forsian likes to fuck so he can see his mate's face. To watch as she comes. To see how he can destroy her for all others. Ruin her. Possess her. Pleasure her."

Oh god, my panties were ruined.

With a hand at the center of my chest, he pushed me back so I lay sprawled across the table. Hooking the backs of my knees, he held me open. His hands slid beneath my butt and tugged my pants down my legs. When he followed to settle on his knees before me, I whimpered.

Quickly he stripped me of everything below the waist, even my boots and socks. And then he put my legs over his shoulders, settled between my parted thighs and looked his fill.

"Mak," I moaned. He hadn't even touched me yet.

"You'll give me this. Your pleasure. I want it all over my face, your scent, your taste, as we go on this mission. And after you come I will lick your desire all up. Only then will I fuck you."

I whimpered, tensed my leg muscles in the hopes of pulling him closer. *There.*

"You want my cock, don't you?" His finger swirled at my entrance and my hips bucked.

"Yes. Please. Anything. Just touch me."

"Ah, you beg so sweetly. I wonder if you taste as sweet."

It was then that he lowered his head. Made me come. Made me forget about everything but his wicked skill to ruthlessly rule my body.

8

Mak, Shuttle 2, The Colony Moon

"Marz, you read?" Gwen sat next to me, in the co-pilot's seat, her hands moving so quickly over the control panel they were nearly a blur. She was in her element. Fast. Deadly.

Beautiful. It was a wonder she'd been grounded, for she was an incredible asset to any mission. An amazing Coalition fighter, and a pilot, which I hadn't known about. To think she had to bargain with the governor to be able to use her expertise was a shame.

Her scent lingered on my skin and it made my cock grow hard. Again. I did not wish to bathe for days so I could hold on to that last connection to her once I left.

"We're here," Marz copied. "We're on foot. Ten minutes to first coordinates."

"Copy that. We're heading out in five. Radio checks every ten."

"Ten minutes. Mark." Marz sounded calm, which was good. I needed to make sure this mission went according to plan, that Gwen and the two Prillon warriors wandering around out there in the moon's fog returned to the planet's surface alive. I might be leaving Gwen behind after this, but while she was with me, I'd ensure her safety.

"Mark." Gwen checked the display on her wrist and looked up, those dark eyes looking at me, but laser-focused on the mission. "Ready?"

Nodding, I looked back out the cockpit display and set our small shuttle down gently, the landing struts taking the weight with a soft groan.

"I will protect you, Gwen, and then I must leave. I can't go back to The Colony."

"I know." She unbuckled and climbed out of her seat to stand, for once, taller than me. She lifted her hands to my face, leaned down and kissed me gently on the lips. Her touch was soft, feminine. It was the lightest touch she'd ever given me, and it rocked me to my core, especially now, knowing her sheer strength. "It's okay, Makarios of Kronos. You don't belong here. I understand that."

She offered me a small smile.

I arched my brow. "Was that a good-bye kiss?"

"Never." She grinned now, giving me another kiss, this one much harder. Faster. And with quite a bit of tongue. My cock stirred, liking this. "You're mine 'til you're dead, right? That's a long time, Mak. Anything can happen."

She moved away, out of reach, before I could argue. I didn't like her words, and if we'd been in my quarters back on The Colony, she'd have been over my knee for it. She was fast, and the seat harness kept me in place when I tried to go after her.

Fuck.

By the time I got the buckles undone, she was in the ready area, helmet on, armed to the teeth with ion blasters, a larger rifle, a line of grenades attached to her belt and a very wicked looking knife strapped to her thigh. A small pack rested on her back, and I knew the Prillon, Vance, would carry an identical bag filled to the top with explosives.

Enough to take out a much larger ship than the small shuttle we'd flown up to the moon's surface. Enough to take out a Hive communications array and dozens of Scouts or Drones. And my Gwen right along with them.

I wanted to tease her, to lighten the mood, but that proved impossible. Odds were, she would need all of the explosives, the weapons. We knew the Hive were out there. And we were stupid enough to be going out into that swirling fog to find them.

"Report." That was Governor Rone's voice coming through the helmet speakers, loud and clear.

"We're exiting the shuttle now. We'll arrive at the first mark in"—Gwen checked the navigation display in her helmet. I saw the objective clearly in my own after I put it on, but I had no desire to talk to Maxim Rone, the uptight Prillon who'd kept me a pseudo-prisoner on The Colony for far too long. He might have been governor, but that didn't mean I had to like him—"about five minutes."

"We're listening, Lieutenant, tracking both teams," he stated, making sure we knew she was being watched. One fuck up on Gwen's part and I had no doubt he'd yank her back to base and ground her again.

"Figured you would."

I raised a brow at her flippant tone, but she just smiled at me through her helmet and hit the control switch that lowered the ramp to the ground. A dense, swirling gray mist enveloped us both, wrapping around us like coils. Instantly, visibility went to just a couple of steps in any direction.

Right away, I was on alert. Not as a fighter, for I wasn't one. Never had been. But as a mate. It might be a new thing, but the protective instincts I felt for Gwen were fierce.

I grabbed her by the arm as she took her first step toward the ground, not hard, just hard enough to get her attention. "Stay where I can see you," I ordered.

My female tilted her head up at me and smiled. It wasn't a sweet smile. "Check your in-helmet display, Mak. You can track me all over this rock. And you might like being bossy in the sack, but here, in this fucking fog, I'm in charge."

Fuck, she was right. I was only here to keep her safe, not run the mission. So I did as she asked, already knowing what I would find. I could, indeed, see a small dot indicating her position relative to mine. Captain Marz and the Prillon Vance showed up on the monitoring display as well. In red, the areas we'd mapped out for ReCon were bright targets laid out over a grid between the two shuttle landing sites.

I didn't care. Blips of color weren't enough.

"No, mate. Stay where I can see you with my own two eyes."

"Mate?" Gwen shrugged off my grip. "That's ridiculous. That's like, three feet."

"I will not argue with you, female."

"Female?"

I should have taken note of Braun's earlier words about Earth females. I should have remembered that they had to be tricked into allowing for their own protection. But my body raged at me to protect her, to stay next to her, to keep her safe. I imagined her hurt, caught by the Hive once again, and my mind seethed. My fangs dropped and my voice was part growl, part hiss. "You will obey me in this. You are mine. I will protect you."

Gwen patted me on the arm, her head tilted to the side, a look of seeming innocence on her face. "Get a grip, fang boy. Not gonna happen."

Before I could argue, she was gone, disappearing into the swirl of fog, nothing more than a small green dot inside my helmet.

"Gods be damned! Gwendolyn. Get back here!" I roared into the microphone, but that little green dot kept moving farther and farther away and at a pace too fast for a normal human.

The husky masculine laughter I knew was coming from base didn't help my mood. Neither did Captain Marz's amused chuckle in my ear.

"Shut the fuck up, Marz. Or I'll remove your arms from your body," I growled.

Now Vance was laughing at me, too.

"Fuck both of you."

And my sweet, docile female's voice chimed in last. "No, Mak, the only person on this planet you get to fuck is me."

The laughter continued, completely at my expense and that only angered me further.

"Gods damn all of you, stay on task and shut the fuck up." The governor's order shut down Marz and Vance's laughter, but I should have known it wouldn't stop my Gwen. That female was too fierce and stubborn for her own good.

Again, advice I should have heeded from Warlord Braun.

"Sorry, Governor," she said sweetly, almost too sweetly. "Just staking my claim on Mak's magnificent cock."

What. The. Fuck?

"Shut it, Lieutenant." The governor meant it, but it was my mate's distant laughter echoing in the background that made me grin. Yeah, that was my mate. That, and the fact that Gwen had just told everyone on the planet that my cock was magnificent. Which it was.

Giving up on taming the wildness out of my female, I followed her little green dot on the helmet display, determined to protect her, whether she wanted my protection or not.

Gwen

I COULDN'T SEE a damn thing... but I could hear them. The Hive. In my head. The subtle vibration of multiple high-ranking Hive Soldiers moving over my flesh, under my skin, like the subtle stroking of a thousand mosquitos' wings hovering over my body, ready to bite. The Hive hadn't given me this technology to use against them, but that's exactly what I was doing now.

They were here. Somewhere. And I had to find them, kill them, before they could hurt Mak again.

When I'd been a prisoner, I'd vowed to fight them until there was nothing left of me. I'd hunt and kill the Hive with my dying breath. But that was my choice. Not Mak's.

All he wanted was his freedom. To get away from all this madness and forget, go back to his old life. To just... fly away.

I couldn't do that, but he could. And I could help him. If I could take out the Hive communications center before he caught sight of them, the deed would be done. He'd be free, and he'd never have to face them again. He wouldn't have to look one of them in the eye and remember what they'd done to him.

It wasn't much, but it was all I could do to help. And I wanted to do something, to know I'd given him a gift, taken care of him in some small way. He might be the one wearing the bossy pants, but I could be in charge here, get shit done. For him.

The urge to protect him was stupid, and territorial, and didn't make any sense, but my heart didn't care. I needed to do this for him. One last thing.

"Gwen, stop. Wait for me. Don't be foolish." Mak's order was easy to ignore.

I ran toward the buzzing, the almost imperceptible hum of my old tormentors. The signal wasn't exactly like I remembered, but then, the specific Nexus Unit that had worked on me, tortured me and began the integrations, who'd made me part of his Hive mind, was far from here in another sector of the galaxy. The Hive Soldiers who were here on the moon must be under the dominion of another Nexus Unit.

Not mine. They called him Nexus 2.

I would never forget it. He'd told me his name as he worked on me, tortured me, changed me to his liking. His real name.

He'd wanted me to stay. To be *his*.

To have his children.

To be his queen.

My stomach churned as I ran toward my past, the horror of those weeks spent in thrall of Nexus 2, fighting the dark depths of his mind, the hypnotic pull of his dark eyes on my emotions. He wasn't like the others the Coalition fought and killed every day. He was an alien race. His skin the darkest blue. His eyes like the black inky depths of a great white shark back on Earth. There was nothing human in those eyes or in his touch. He wasn't a drone, wasn't what the Coalition thought of as the Hive, the warriors from other worlds controlled by biosynthetic integrations and psychic frequencies. The ones who traveled in threes.

No. Nexus 2—my Hive nemesis—was something else. One of the Hive core. He controlled millions, perhaps billions of minds. And he'd wanted mine. He'd wanted me to give myself to him willingly.

As if.

"Lieutenant, where are you going?" Governor Rone's voice was in my ear now. "You are off the grid."

"We were wrong. They're here. I'm close. I can hear them."

Radio silence, then all of them were yelling at me at once.

"Stand down, now! Wait for backup."

The governor. Yeah, ummm, no on that.

"No, Gwen! You will not. I forbid it."

Forbid? Sorry, Mak. I don't know that word.

"We're twenty minutes from your location. Wait for us!"

Marz. Wait? That might be smart, but then they'd all want to play, and I wanted to kill every single one of the Hive bastards myself. To be done with them, until the next mission. To keep Mak safe on this one so he could be free.

"What the fuck are you doing, female?" That was Vance, and he was the only one who said anything worth responding to.

"I'm going to kill me some Hive, that's what I'm doing." I checked my timer, took stock of the level of buzzing inside my head. "You should arrive in time for clean-up, boys. I'll try not to make too big of a mess." *Lie.* I was going to stain the ground with their Hive blood like a warrior goddess. "I'm out."

"No!"

I turned off my radio. Seriously, did not need to hear all the shouting or have them pick up on anything I said or did.

I had an advantage, something none of them knew. Not Marz, not Vance, not Mak and not even the governor. Something I'd never admitted. Not when the Intelligence Core questioned me for days after I showed up alone in that Hive ship. Not when the doctors poked and prodded me for hours, running hundreds of tests. Not when I looked into Mak's eyes and felt the urge to reveal the truth I carried to someone I trusted.

But I kept my secret, because Mak wasn't mine. Not really. We'd made a bargain. Fucked and agreed that we would go our separate ways. He was leaving The Colony. Leaving me. Therefore, he didn't need to know.

Shoulders set, I did the one thing I hadn't let myself do since I escaped the Nexus who tried to own me. I went full Hive. Yeah, it was a thing, a thing I had a feeling others on The Colony couldn't do. It was like being Bruce Banner and going all Incredible Hulk. No one—at least no one but those from Earth—would understand that reference. In alien-speak, it was like going Atlan Beast, but better. I was already ridiculously strong. I didn't need to let the beast out. I needed to let the *Hive* out. Or, let them into my mind. Into my body. I could use their technology, their plans for me against them. I'd connect to the Hive Soldiers I now knew I'd find over the next rise on the lunar surface.

The buzzing in my head went from dull ache to chainsaw scream in a matter of seconds, but I just gritted my teeth and didn't fight the flow of information they were giving me. I was like a moving super-computer, processing on-the-fly data and information. Running toward them, I filtered out what I could around the massive migraine making my eyes feel like they were literally about to pop free from their sockets.

A warm dribble of liquid slid from my nose to my lip and I tasted blood. My brain was literally full. Overflowing.

So be it.

I ran faster, as fast as the bio-synth fibers in my new body allowed. And I was fast, rocks and dust flying under my feet as I passed the landscape in a complete blur. The faster I got to them, the faster the pain would stop, the mission would be finished. I'd take the fuckers down.

Just as I'd anticipated, the Hive were waiting, lined up, three-by-three in triangle formation. Nine in total, they all had their weapons pointed at me as I came to a dead stop a few steps before them and cleared my throat. I wasn't winded at all, yet adrenaline coursed through my veins, making me shake, making my heart race too fast. I would have worried about it bursting, but it wasn't wholly human anymore either.

I didn't need to say any words aloud, knew they were linked to me telepathically, just as I was now linked to them.

But I spoke regardless, needed the sound to ground me to reality, remind myself that I was more than just a Hive integration.

"We are Nexus 2. Report. Why have you not finished here?" I was careful to speak as a true Hive even though it sounded ridiculous. As part of the complete entity known as Nexus 2, as part of my supposed Hive master, I never would have referred to myself as singular. No Hive did, except the solo Nexus units that controlled the entire Hive collective. The Hive 'bosses.' The dark blue creatures were terrifying, and so powerful with their telepathy they could convince a woman she was standing in a field of butterflies and wildflowers while she was undergoing surgery. Could make her feel affection, even love, with no basis or knowledge that it wasn't real. Yeah, that had been fun. *Not.*

Until later. Waking up with Nexus 2 out of telepathic range had been an agony of self-hatred that I never wished to repeat. In fact, seeing the nine Hive Soldiers before me made my skin crawl and my stomach churn with acid.

While I'd been afraid of the Nexus units, these Hive were underlings to me. To them, I was *their* superior. Confirming this, all nine dropped to one knee before me and I took advantage, scanning their minds for intent, orders, anything I could glean from them. And sad as it was, I touched their minds with my own, looking for one of them still fighting, worthy of being saved. A Coalition fighter who still fought the Hive mind control and just hadn't been lucky enough to escape, to exist on The Colony.

The highest-ranking Soldier was once Prillon. Covered from head to toe, not one inch of skin remained untouched by silver Hive technology. He looked like an android, nothing biological or natural left. He spoke aloud, as I had done, and I realized the Hive hadn't been able to hear me through my closed helmet. I couldn't hear his voice above a soft mumble. But I heard him inside my head.

"My queen, we are to protect the communication array until Nexus 4 is complete in his task." Complete? I'd heard that term used before. That was Hive code for stealing a female, forcing her to endure Hive implantation and breeding, Hive Nexus mind control, and becoming 'one' with the Nexus who tormented her.

"And what of the transporter resources? Have they been secured?" I'd been in on several meetings where the possibility of the Hive stealing the mineral mined on The Colony, the substance used to make our transport systems work, had been discussed. If the Hive took enough to cripple Coalition operations, they would win the war. Despite months of searching, we hadn't been able to find them—led by Nexus 4—in the network of caves beneath the planet's surface. Didn't even know if that was, in fact, what they were doing sulking around like sewer rats underground. And we knew they were there, just like Krael, the traitor, who was with them.

"The first shipment was received. The second shipment is scheduled to depart as soon as Nexus 4 gives us the command."

Great. So they'd already stolen enough mineral from the mines on The Colony for a full shipment with another ready to go. "And what is the delay? We are not pleased with the delay."

The Hive Soldiers shuddered at the tone of my voice. As a female linked to a Nexus unit, I could torture them with my mind alone. I was a queen bee in a hive of soldiers and drones. I could quite literally kill any one of them on a whim if the mood struck... and I was definitely in the mood. Everything personal might have been stripped from these Coalition fighters when they were turned, but they did know fear. They still had an instinct for survival. Not even the Hive programming could drive that primal instinct from their bodies. And fear was an emotion that served everyone well if they wanted to remain alive. Or at least functional to the Hive.

"Nexus 4 has not been successful in securing a female."

I swallowed down the bile that had crept into my throat. I knew very well what it was like to be a *secured* female. Nexus 2 had taught me well. The dark blue alien creature had wanted me as his mate, his queen. And I'd nearly lost my mind, all sense of self, under his control. A mile-wide stubborn streak, the same one that got me into so much trouble when I was a little girl—hell, still got me in trouble with the governor—had saved me. I simply refused to stop fighting until finally, my chance came, and I stole a ship and escaped.

"We demand the exact location of Nexus 4. We will speak to him directly," I said, continuing with my use of plural-speak.

I'd kill these nine, then return to the planet surface and take out the rest of them. And Nexus 4, the telepathic Nexus unit who'd tried to murder CJ's and Rezzer's twins a few months ago? Tried to take Caroline Jane for himself? Kill Rezzer's Alan children already growing strong and healthy in CJ's womb? Was the Nexus still down there? Hunting for another female? There weren't too many women on The Colony—the Nexus wouldn't care if she were single or mated—which meant bad things for my Earth friends. And I knew Rezzer would most likely go into beast mode if given the chance to join me in a little payback.

I'd give that dark blue asshole a female, all right, just not the easily tortured variety he was counting on. A taste of his own medicine was in order.

The Hive Soldier before me stood, slowly. "Nexus 4 has agreed to meet with you. He will petition you to ally with him, as Nexus 2 is not here to oversee your care."

It took me a moment to understand what he was saying. That Nexus 4 wanted to be my Hive *protector*. What a load of bullshit. Breeder was more like it. Jesus.

Were the damn Hive no different about females than the aliens on the planet below? Since my so-called mate, Nexus 2, was in another sector of space and not standing beside me, Nexus 4 felt the need to steal me for himself? For my own protection? To oversee my *care?* To keep me... what, safe?

Torture was more like it. Forced breeding of more little blue sociopaths. No.

But then I knew one thing that I *had* told the Intelligence Core doctors. The Nexus units weren't friends. Hell, they hated one another, saw each other as a temporary yet necessary evil, allies and bodies needed to defeat the Coalition Fleet and conquer the galaxy.

But once that was done, they'd turn on each other like starving monsters fighting over meat. Each Nexus unit controlled a specific sector of space, their own Scouts and Soldiers. They were in a race to assimilate every biological being into their personal armies for when the *real* war started, the war between the Nexus units themselves.

For centuries, everyone in the Coalition of Planets believed that the Hive was an organized collective of cooperative thinkers. The Intelligence Core, and the few who knew the Nexus units existed, had believed they were brothers in truth. Aliens bound to a single cause, under one banner.

They were wrong. The Nexus units were singular. Selfish. They cooperated because they had to in order to survive an organized Coalition Fleet. A united resistance. Cooperation was expedient. Nothing more. Nothing less.

The Coalition worlds? Raw material. We were supplies to be acquired. Warriors to be added to the Hive tally. Bullets in a gun. Bodies. Expendable.

And the Nexus units would not hesitate to steal another's Soldiers or Scouts, or me. As far as I knew, I was the first fully integrated Nexus *mate*.

I couldn't wait to kill Nexus 4. They were all the same to me. Pure evil. Without a conscience. Without a soul. I just needed to remember not to look into his eyes before I got the job done. One look into those dark depths, and I'd be done. Trapped. Completely under his control. Because while I was balls-to-the-wall tough thanks to them, I had one weakness, one way they could gain control over me against my will.

Connection. Mind to mind connection.

If I let Nexus 4 in, I was done. Mind fucked. It would be o-v-e-r.

"Send us the coordinates," I commanded. "We will go to him now."

"Yes, my queen." The information streamed into my head like a data upload and I pushed deeper, gaining access to more information than he intended to give me. Like taking candy from a baby. I received the location of the ship on the lunar surface. Maps of their hidden dens on The Colony. Coordinate numbers. Mining sites. Positions of Hive

Soldiers and Drones. I had all of it in seconds, including the location of their waiting Nexus cargo ship and the amount of stolen mineral in the ship's hold. In a matter of two seconds, it was all mine.

"Thank you." Smiling now, I walked to him and grabbed his head, helmet and all. Twisting with all the rage I'd held in check the past weeks, I cracked his neck and dropped him, dead, at my feet. I felt nothing in the action. There was no Prillon left in that body. Had I met him in the past, I was sure he'd want me to kill him, to end him, knowing he'd never want to be like this, his mind gone, nothing left but a shell forced to do evil.

Shocked and surprised, the others hurried to rise from their kneeling positions and fire their weapons.

The first ion blast stung more than I thought it would, but not enough to stop me from cracking the offender's ribcage, forcing the bones inward until his heart stopped beating. He'd been Viken once. Now, he was a monster. A dead monster.

Two down, seven to go.

Pulling out the knife strapped to my thigh, I cut the throat of the integrated Atlan closest to me. He was still on his knees. His eyes glazed over and I swear I saw gratitude there. He didn't fight or try to stop me, which broke my heart, hurt in a million different ways. He looked too much like Mak. Too big. Too strong. Too noble.

He could have killed me, but he'd fought the conditioning, held himself still for the killing blow. Yes, *this* was what I had expected. Some hint of life, of the original being within.

The relief in his eyes would haunt my dreams forever. He was finally at peace.

The injustice of his sacrifice made me want to scream

and cry my eyes out. But that wouldn't do any good. He wanted to die, to have dignity. Honor. He deserved no less.

An ion blast hit me from behind and I turned into the line of fire with a smile.

I was Nexus now, thanks to their own masters. They would need a lot more than their ion blasters to take me down. They were shooting a pellet gun at an angry bear.

Evidently figuring that out, three of them rushed me and I took them down with an arcing roundhouse kick that would have made Chuck Norris proud. The kick broke the first Soldier's skull, shattered the second's ribcage and took off the bottom half of the third's leg. He fell to the ground with a scream of pain, which went silent as I stomped on his neck.

I faced the others, striking without mercy until I stood alone surrounded by the dead. The entire encounter had only taken a couple of minutes, but I felt like I'd been fighting for years—because I had. I'd wanted to go on missions, to destroy the Hive one at a time, but it was never easy. Never without personal pain. Emotional destruction.

I needed a valium. Xanax. Something to make me forget.

Mak had accomplished that; for a few stolen hours I'd been something other than a broken thing, a Hive queen, a mate of the blue Nexus bastard who'd wanted me to carry his children. Mak made me feel alive. Beautiful. Sensual. *Me.*

But not wanted. Sexually, definitely, but not completely. Not the way my broken heart needed. He refused to bite me, refused to even consider staying with me and living on The Colony. Once the Intelligence Core figured out the truth I'd kept from them—and what I'd just collected in my head—they'd want to use me to lure and capture the Nexus units that controlled the Hive. They'd want to transport me all over the galaxy. I'd be bait to lure the Nexus to them, over and over. It made sense; I couldn't fault them for the plan. Hell, it was a good idea, although I wasn't excited about being the lure at their whim. I wasn't sure I'd survive it, and I wasn't sure I wanted to.

I'd just be... living. Surviving. Fighting. No happiness. No joy. No connection other than through the minds of other Hive. And that wasn't the connection I craved.

Without Mak, I'd be just like the Atlan I just killed. A former shell of myself in a body that was no longer my own. Used for battle, for fighting. For strategy and nothing more. I would be a pawn in the fighting cog that was spread out over the entire galaxy.

I couldn't live with that. Not for long. Not if I couldn't have the only male I wanted. It had only been a day since I'd chosen him, since we'd made the bargain. But so much had happened since then. The *connection*—yes, that word kept repeating in my head over and over—was powerful. Intense. It was as if we *had* been matched through the Brides Program. Or were marked mates from Everis. The bond was real, and he hadn't even claimed me. I had to wonder what it would be like if he did make me truly his.

Powerful. Intense. Just... peaceful.

Yet Makarios of Kronos was a wild thing, a free spirit. He had not promised anything. Had not gone back on his word, nor behaved dishonorably. I couldn't fault him for anything except hooking my emotions in a way I never anticipated. But that was my problem, not his. I would not be a shackle around his ankle. I would honor our bargain.

But I knew nothing would help except striking at the

heart of the Hive itself. At their core. At the Nexus minds that controlled them all.

And Nexus 4 hiding on the planet's surface like a snake? He'd know I was coming. Which was just fine with me.

Walking toward the Hive ship I intended to pilot to my meeting with Nexus 4, I allowed the Hive tech that nearly covered my body to return to its original color—the better to tempt the Nexus unit with—a dark, vibrant blue. I'd learned to hold it off, but now, like a dam breaking, the color washed over me. I looked just like him now. The way Nexus 2 had made me.

Blue. Feminine. Strong.

Perfect for breeding.

If there was one urge as primal as survival, it was the urge to fuck. And as far as I knew, I was the only female in the galaxy custom designed to tempt the blue bastards. If I could get him thinking with his cock instead of his head, I'd have a chance. And instead of touching him with lover's hands, I'd rip his head right off.

9

Mak, Surface of The Colony Moon

I'M OUT?

Was that what Gwen had actually said to me? I was going to find that female, put her over my knee, and spank her ass until it burned red under my palm.

I'm out.

No. She'd be spanked, and then I'd be inside her, fucking her into submission, making sure she never did anything this stupid again. When I'd sat in the mission briefing, I'd said I'd keep Gwen safe. Yes, it had been a ruse to get me off the fucking planet, but I'd told the truth. While she was with me, I'd keep her safe.

And then she went off and did this. What the fuck?

She could be off on her own being killed by the fucking Hive right now. And she had a bag full of explosives strapped to her back.

FUCK.

The thought of her dying, being blown to bits, had me running faster, screaming at Marz and Vance to hurry the fuck up.

"We're closer to our ship," Marz replied. "We'll run back and fly to her last known location."

"Just hurry the fuck up, Marz."

"We're coming, Mak. Just keep her alive." I heard his pissed off tone. While I had no doubt he'd want to spank Gwen for her behavior too, he'd just have to be satisfied knowing I took her in hand.

I just had to keep her alive until then.

Easier said than done. If this was how the governor thought he would control my female, he had failed. Miserably. No doubt he was following every second of this clusterfuck through the sat-comm. What had I been thinking? I could never leave her under his protection. She was too damn stubborn. Too strong-willed. Too fierce for her own good. And the way she'd run off—with her ridiculous Hive speed—into the swirling fog and toward the enemy, was proof of that.

Warlord Braun's advice on human females haunted me yet again. I had not understood the weight of his words, the depth of understanding he had gained about these females. Fierce didn't begin to describe them. And mine, with Cyborg integrations... I was fucked.

These females charged into battle with no thought for their own survival. And even if Gwen was not officially my mate, the fact that I could not mate and bite her would not stop me from protecting her from herself. I was a male of honor, and whether she liked it or not, she had given herself to me. Submitted to my care. Submitted to my cock. She was mine.

I shut off my helmet's relay, the line of communication back to mission control, back to the planet's surface. There were some things I didn't want to share, including whatever the fuck set Gwen off.

I smelled them before I saw them, the metallic tang of Hive who survived on their strange mixture of nutrient shakes and electrical charges, who did not sweat or cry or *feel*.

My Hyperion fangs burst free, not to mate, but to rip and tear flesh from bone. To fight.

I scented Hive. And my female was among them. Fighting. Alone.

Never again.

With a roar of challenge, I leaped over the small rise to find devastation, and Gwen standing, untouched, in the center of one, two, three... six, no nine dead Hive Soldiers. One of them so big he had obviously been an Atlan.

The sight made me tremble. She'd taken them on alone. All of them. Nine fucking enemies.

When she turned to look at me, her eyes swirled a dark, impenetrable blue, the color one I'd never seen before. Not her own. Alien. Like her face, her hands... blue. But the way she was looking at me was a punch to my gut, so filled with agony and betrayal. I doubted she knew how much she revealed to me in that gaze, but I knew her. Had been inside her.

Loved her. Fuck. I loved her. I'd die for her. Never leave her.

If she'd have me. It took almost losing her to realize that.

And after only a day. When I thought now that she was

mine, I wasn't just a protective male. No, I was so much more. My heart was involved.

"Go, Makarios," she said. "Take the ship we arrived in and go home. You are free." Turning away from me, she removed her helmet and shook out her black hair, letting it fall down her back. The toxic chemicals that swirled in the air around us seemed to have no effect on her. She wasn't gasping for breath. No warning signals came through my helmet because of her diagnostics. Nothing. And thankfully I'd shut comms down. I didn't need the governor hearing this conversation, knowing I'd planned to take a ship and go back to Rogue 5.

"Gwen? What are you doing?" I took a step closer to grab the helmet and shove it back on her head. "Put that back on."

She turned to face me, unzipping her uniform as she did so. She stepped out of everything as I just watched. Transfixed. Stunned. Confused. After a minute, she stood naked before me, the strange fog swirling around her body like whispers caressing her skin.

Frozen in place, I stared. I couldn't look away. She was beautiful, yet not the same Gwen I knew. Vibrant, deep blue from head to toe, her black hair formed a dark halo around her curves. The blue was divided into sections of color, forming a pattern of light and dark I longed to trace with my hands. My lips.

By the gods. What the fuck had the Hive done to her?

"Go, Mak. We had a deal. You're free." She repeated her words, but I still couldn't move. Or look away. Like I'd be able to leave her now. Naked and blue with dead Hive littered around her feet.

"And where are you going? What do you think you're doing, female?"

She tilted her head, her smile sad. "Killing as many of them as I can." Moving slightly, her head rotated as if she were listening to something I couldn't hear. "He's angry with me for killing his Soldiers. Good." She was grinning now, the sight almost frightening. All she needed was a flaming sword or serpents coming out of her head and warriors on dozens of worlds would build shrines and worship her. "We must go now. He is waiting."

I frowned. "Who is we? Who is waiting? What the fuck is going on? Why the fuck did you take your clothes off?" Moving closer, I stopped her from walking away with a hand on her bare shoulder. "Gwen. Talk to me. Please. I'll help you."

She shook her head, her black hair sliding like silky rope. "You can't help me." Her blue hand rested on top of mine, her naked body so perfect I felt like I was talking to a statue carved by an artisan. Where was my mate? My Gwen? And who was this creature looking up at me with such resignation in her eyes?

"I can, if you'll tell me what you're doing." I'd never talked to her so softly. We'd been all fire and stubbornness, a battle of wills, fighting and fucking until we both were finally sated.

But this? Her, now? I didn't understand and there was no fucking way I'd be leaving her side.

She blinked, slowly, and I would swear I could see her mind calculating her options. "I'm taking the Hive ship to the surface and killing Nexus 4 before he can take another shipment of transport minerals off the planet."

Nexus 4 on the planet's surface? Minerals? Whatever.

Other people could work on that problem. She could tell the governor and the thousands of restless warriors on the surface the details, let them deal with it. And they would. Eagerly. I didn't give a shit about any of them, or the Hive, or how furious the governor was going to be. Only her.

"Alone?"

She looked at me as if I were the crazy one, standing naked on a moon. "Of course. The rest of you would never get close enough to touch him." Her smile was frightening, full of death and menace. Not human. "He will want this body. He will not be able to resist what the other created for him."

Let her get close enough to *touch* a Nexus 4, who or whatever the fuck that was? Naked? To tempt him into *touching her?*

"Over my dead body."

"Go, Mak. You are free." She shrugged out of my hold and resumed walking. Quickly.

Running after her, I swept her up into my arms and held her against my chest, exactly as I'd done when carrying her to my quarters to lick and taste and fuck her. I wanted her to remember *that*. I *needed* her to remember us. But I was in this damn space suit, so I couldn't kiss her. Taste her.

But I could touch her, to get her out of her head like I had in my bed. Up against my wall. Oh yeah, I'd wiped all thoughts from her head, and I wished I could do that now.

"Let me go," she struggled, but for once I would use all of my strength to keep her right where I wanted. She could hurt me, force me to fight her with all my strength. I saw the knowledge in her eyes, but she didn't. Which made my heart skip a beat. She cared, at least that much.

"You'll have to kill me, Gwen. You're not going alone."

She froze in my arms, the glazed look finally leaving her eyes. Anger flared. Good, I could deal with anger. "That's not fair, Mak. We had a deal. You're supposed to go. Go home to Rogue 5 and Kronos. So, do it. Leave."

"No." I wound my gloved hand into her mass of black hair and held her still, tilting her head back so she would have to either look at me or close her eyes like a coward. And I knew she had courage to spare.

"God damn it." Her eyes shimmered with unshed tears and I wished I could kiss them away. My fierce warrior was no more. I did not like that she was reduced to tears, but I would not let her go until this was settled, until she understood I wasn't leaving her side.

"What are you doing? You don't want a mate, remember? So, go."

"I want *you*."

She shook her head. She heard me but wasn't really listening. "No." Her gaze darted down to my elongated fangs, then back up to my eyes. "No, Mak. You don't. Not forever."

The bite. Gods be damned, she thought I didn't want her because I didn't bite her as a Hyperion would. Hadn't claimed her. Her upset, these tears were all because of me. "My bite would kill you, Gwen. I am half Forsian. The combination of the Hyperion and Forsian genetic lines makes my bite toxic to a mate. There are only three half-breeds like me in existence, and the last male who tried to claim a female could not resist the instinct to bite. He watched her die in his arms."

She tried to push against my hold as I heard the rumble of Marz and Vance's shuttle landing nearby.

"That's bullshit," she countered. "You should have told

me. I'm not exactly normal, Mak." She motioned down to her startlingly blue body, the fact that she wasn't wearing a helmet either. Or anything, for that matter. She took a deep breath and blew it out into the swirling fog to emphasize her point.

I told her the truth, but it didn't mean I would bite her. Ever.

"How is it that you can breathe this air?" I asked, changing the subject. No one should be able to do that. Even the Hive she'd killed had been wearing helmets.

"I'm not exactly human anymore, in case you didn't notice."

I looked her over, taking my time, making sure she would see the desire building in my eyes. "I don't care what color your skin is, mate. Blue or orange, red or purple, makes no difference to me. You are beautiful. And you're mine. I'm not letting you go."

Footsteps sounded behind me, but I ignored the two Prillon as they approached. Gwen, however, was not as lucky, flinching at their words.

"By the gods."

"What the fuck?"

Scowling, I turned and snapped my fangs at the two males. "Do you dare insult my mate? And get your fucking comms units turned off," I growled, not wanting them to capture any of this for others to know about.

Marz put his hands to his helmet, then in front of him, palms out. "Done," he said. "And insult your mate? No. Never. But what the hell happened to you, Gwen? Are you all right? Why are you blue? Where's your armor? Do we need to call medical? We can have you back to the surface and in a med station in no time."

"I'm fine."

Vance walked around me and whistled low, taking in the dead Hive bodies lying on the ground a small distance away. "You do this, Mak?"

"No. I did not. And you insult my mate by considering me first."

"Holy fuck." Marz joined Vance, looking around. He bent over to inspect one of the bodies, blatantly ignoring the fact that Gwen was naked. As if this were a normal occurrence on a mission. "Remind me not to piss you off again, Lieutenant."

Gwen's burst of laughter was music to my ears. She sounded like herself again. Better than that, she relaxed in my arms, content to allow me to hold her. Even though she was still blue, she was still mine.

Would always be mine.

I looked down into her eyes. "Now that the team is here, tell us what the plan is."

"There is no us, Mak," she replied.

"The hell there's not." Marz's tone was full command mode. He outranked both of us, and he was not shy about reminding Gwen of that fact. "Talk to me, Lieutenant. Tell me exactly what the *fuck* is going on here. And why the fuck are you naked?"

With a sigh I knew was surrender, I wrapped my arms around her body the best I could to cover her. Thankfully, Marz and Vance both had the good sense not to look anywhere but at Gwen's face, which saved me from the need to bash in their skulls.

She recounted everything she'd learned from the Hive she'd killed, including the part where she could talk to them telepathically, which was fucking insane. I'd seen the integrations the Hive had made, up close and personal, but we were all now learning the sheer extent of what they'd done to her. More than any of us ever even imagined. Probably so much more than the intake doctor had even known. She was fucking blue. When she was finished, we all stood in silence. Shocked.

Numb.

And deep within, the Hyperion beast paced in his cage, biding his time. Waiting to kill.

Vance was seated on a rock, tapping his ion blaster against his thigh. "Shouldn't we tell the governor? At least let him know what we're going to do?"

My mate fought my hold and I let her stand, let her pace before us, glorious, beautiful, and naked. She had no modesty, no shame, and so I sat back and admired what was mine. When I suggested she cover up, put her armor back on, the scowl she'd given me shut me down instantly. "It's covered in blood, Mak."

I didn't like the idea of Marz or Vance seeing her, but unless I wrestled her to the ground and covered her up forcefully—which wouldn't get me anywhere with her—I'd just have to resign myself to the fact that those males could look, but would never, *ever* touch.

She was fierce and I had no hope of controlling her. Each sway of her hips, every rock she crumbled to dust with her bare hand, was a reminder of that. A trail of dust clung to her feet from the rocks she'd pulverized as she paced. Thinking.

Gods, she was strong. Stronger than anyone I'd ever seen. Man. Beast. Atlan or Hive.

And she'd given herself to me. Let me hold her down. Fuck her. Fill her with my seed. Eat her pussy. Conquer her body. *Let me.* Because if she hadn't really wanted me, there would have been no way for me to do any of it. She was too powerful in her own right. And yet...

Mine.

I ached to toss her over my shoulder, carry her to the nearest boulder large enough to bend her over and fuck her. Hard.

"Mak, you still with me?"

Telling my cock to stop tormenting me, I lifted my head and answered my female. The plan she laid out for us was dangerous. Deadly. Insane. And she was fully prepared to do it alone.

"Always, mate."

"Good." Gwen clapped her hands together and pointed at Marz and Vance. "You two take the two shuttles back to Base 3. Get Rezz. Tell him what's going on. Just Rezzer. No one else. You have a locator beacon?"

"Of course." Marz reached into his pockets and tossed her the small device. She caught it easily.

"Good. Give Rezz the frequency to this beacon and tell him to be ready to move. Tell him we'll meet him at the beacon's location. Got it?"

Marz nodded, even though he was the one in charge, he was quietly taking orders. "Warlord Rezzer deserves vengeance for what the Hive Nexus attempted to do to his mate and children. He may not want to come alone. The other warlords may request to join him."

"Too many cooks spoil the soup," she replied, although I had no idea what the hell that meant. "And I don't want the governor to find out what we're doing until it's too late. He can't know until it's over and I'm long gone."

"Gone? Gone where? You'll have to answer to him eventually. The Intelligence Core will have you in debriefing for weeks." Captain Marz dared argue with her. I let him. He was saying everything I was thinking. Let him be the one to anger my female.

"The Hive ship you see behind me is mine. This is only one Nexus unit, on one world. There at least eight others."

"And you want to hunt them all?" I asked. I knew the answer, but I asked anyway. Where she went, I went. End of discussion. If she wanted to spend the rest of her life hunting Hive, I would be at her side, bashing skulls and killing as many of the bastards as I could.

Gwen turned to look at me, her eyes still blue, not her natural, soft brown. But the determination was easy to recognize. "Yes."

"All right."

Her jaw dropped. "No argument? No chest-beating, caveman protests? Aren't you going to *forbid* me from leaving you? From hunting? From putting myself in danger?"

"No, mate. Where you go, I follow. If you want to hunt and kill a thousand Hive, you will hunt, but you will not do it alone."

"By the gods, will you two shut the fuck up? You're talking about stealing a Hive ship, disobeying the governor's orders and going rogue." Captain Marz paced now, frustration evident in the quick steps and stiffness in his spine.

10

Despite Captain Marz's irritation, Vance sat on the ground, one leg propped up, one flat out in front of him. Completely at ease. "Once the Hive on the planet are taken care of, I don't much care what you two do or where you go, especially since you have this... blue thing going for you. Marz is right, they'll never let you go. But we all agree the threat to The Colony gets taken care of first. And I think we should take a full force of warriors into the caves."

Gwen was shaking her head before Vance finished. "This is not a normal battle. This is a Nexus unit. He'll feel every mind approaching. Know we're coming. If there are too many, he'll run and hide again. I have to go in alone, take out his protection, subdue him so we can finish him once and for all. Once I have him down, Rezzer can come in and do whatever he wants. I'll give him that because I know his experience with the Nexus unit still eats him up on the inside. But I don't want the governor to know. Ever."

"That's treason," Captain Marz cleared his throat. "Punishable by death."

She glanced down at her blue body, then back up at us. "If the Intelligence Core finds out what I am to the Hive, that I have more integrations than they ever imagined, that the Nexus units will come out of hiding to pursue me, to claim me for their own—"

Gwen paused at the growl that rumbled in my throat but glanced away as quickly as she had turned to me, trusting me to pull myself together. No, demanding I do so.

"They'll put me in a cage, Marz. This is why I'm naked, to show you what I'm really like, what they *really* did to me. I'm not normal. I'm not even *normal* for The Colony. I'll be an experiment at best and a weapon at the worst. I won't survive it. You saw me going crazy, grounded on the planet. I'm not just contaminated. I'm something else. I am one of them. Not a drone or a soldier. They made me Nexus. I'm permanently broken. Wrong. At first, I thought I could just do missions and kill Hive and be happy. But that had been unrealistic. I won't be able to hide who I am now. *What* I am now. I can never go home. Hell, I don't even have a home. Once I finish off Nexus 4 and the governor and the others learn the truth, I will have to flee. Escape. And you two must make an oath never to reveal what you saw here today. You can't tell anyone the truth about me." She waved her hand in front of her body. "Do you understand?"

Marz stopped his pacing and turned to face her. "You want to kill the Hive here, then leave us all to go hunt them on your own." He shook his head. "You may be the strongest female I have ever encountered, but you are still a female.

Every cell in my body demands you be protected, not sent into battle. I don't like it."

"You don't have to like it. I'm not asking, Marz. I'm telling you." The threat was there, the fact that she would use force, if necessary, to get through his thick Prillon skull.

"She won't be alone. She is mine." A fact.

Marz looked from Gwen to me, then lifted his head as if to inspect the stars. "May the gods have mercy on us all. They'll throw me in the brig for this."

"Not if they don't know what happened," Vance offered. "Rezzer will keep his mouth shut. We'll get him and Braun to back up our story. We returned to the surface, had an itch to go looking for some trouble in the caves, and got lucky." Vance glanced at my mate, the woman I would die to protect. "We'll tell them you died up here with the Hive." He glanced over to me. "Both of you. Shot off into space. Lost."

Marz looked as if he were about to protest, but he locked his gaze with Vance and slowly nodded. "As long as we destroy the Nexus unit and stop the transport mineral from leaving the surface. We fail"—he turned back to Gwen—"and no more deals. No secrets. We stop them, or every warrior on the planet helps us take them out."

"Done. Agreed." Gwen spoke for herself, which meant she also spoke for me. "But I'm the only one who can get close enough to kill him." Gwen pointed to the Hive ship we could all see outlined not far from where we talked. The dead bodies had been left behind, and the Hive ship was only a few steps away, the odd configuration drifting in and out of view as the fog shifted and moved around us. "Once Nexus 4 is dead, I'm taking their ship, with their flight codes, and I'm going to hunt them and kill them for as long as I can."

I knew Braun. Rezzer. Tane. I knew the few Atlans on this world, and not one would sit out this fight, even if they had to keep their mouths shut and defy orders to be involved. That left Marz and Vance. As Prillons, they were the unknown. The governor was a Prillon as well, and a good leader. But for Gwen, and for Rezzer, this was personal. I understood that now, and I would assist my mate in any way I could, because killing the Nexus was the only way to keep her safe.

"Rezzer will not want to miss this fight," I agreed. "Nor will he come alone. It is his right to accept or decline the presence of the other warlords. It is the beast in him that must decide. But it will be on you, Marz, to make sure he understands what's at stake and keeps his mouth shut."

"Or stays out of it," Gwen added. "I am more than happy to kill Nexus 4 on my own. I am willing to do this for him, and for CJ, and the twins. That is all."

I held my breath as Marz made his decision. Vance was his second, and I knew the other Prillon warrior would support Marz in any decision he made.

He nodded once. "Very well. I will agree to keeping this a secret. *For now.* But if they catch sight of you blue... well, I think the secret will be out. Are you stuck blue now?"

"No. I have full control of my integrations." As she spoke, the blue began to fade until she stood before me as I remembered her, caramel skin, black hair, dark brown eyes I would be happy drowning in.

Marz and Vance wisely looked away. "Fine. Whatever. But there is too much at stake," Marz said. "This information about the Nexus units could turn the tide of the war."

What Marz said was true, but I glanced at Gwen to see if she agreed.

"I already told the Intelligence Core the truth about the Nexus and the nature of their alliance with one another. I am the only secret, Marz. I don't want to be a science experiment, or bait. I can turn the tide of the war all by myself if you all will just let me." She offered a negligent shrug of her shoulders and I couldn't help but enjoy the way her breasts rose and fell with the action. I glanced at the others, ready to poke their eyes out if they noticed the motion. If they had, they made no reaction, their heads still turned like honorable males. Thank fuck.

"So, are we good?" she continued.

"No, I am not good. Maxim deserves vengeance as well. Where this Nexus unit is, the traitor Krael will be, too. He murdered my second, Perro. He nearly killed the governor and murdered the human, Captain Brooks. I do not like this, but I will agree... if you give me and the governor the location of the traitor." Marz held out a hand to Vance, pulling his second up off the ground.

"I second this request," Vance added. "I was not thinking clearly until now. Rezzer is not the only warrior on this planet who deserves vengeance."

Gwen smiled and bowed slightly. "You drive a tough bargain, Marz, but it just so happens that the transport ship and the Nexus unit are not in the same set of caves." She walked to Marz and held out her right hand in the oddly human way they had of making bargains. "I'll *offer* the governor coordinates to the stolen minerals on that cargo ship, for a price."

"What price?" Marz scowled at her.

"That is between him and me. Do we have a deal?"

"You are a formidable female. And yes, we do." Marz placed his gloved hand in hers and she squeezed his hand, shaking his arm up and down in the human ritual. Marz ignored me, which was fine. He released Gwen's hand and spoke to Vance. "You get back to Mak and Gwen's shuttle. Report that there was a battle and we lost track of both Mak and the lieutenant." He turned to me now. "Since your mate's helmet and tracking device is already on the ground, you'll need to dump yours as well, before you leave the moon's surface. The governor has to believe you've been taken by the Hive. That should buy us the time you both need to get into position."

"Done." Smart. I couldn't think right now. Nearly losing Gwen and now watching her stand fearless and proud among us made my cock hard and my chest ache.

"Good. I'll make sure I take plenty of footage of the dead Hive and the scene of the battle. Vance will help me load up the bodies. I'm sure those warriors have family that would like to know their final fates. We'll take them back to The Colony for processing and you two disappear." He looked at Gwen. "You have my private comm code?"

"Of course."

"Use it when you're ready to offer the governor your bargain. How long do I have to recruit Rezzer and the other Atlan Warlords?"

Gwen tilted her head, taking her turn to stare up into the stars. "I'll give you two hours to have them at the cave entrance. Not one minute more. Take a shuttle and head north of Base 3 about eighty miles to the entrance of the ice caves."

"That close?" Vance seemed to pale behind his helmet.

Gwen ignored him. "And tell Rezzer that if I didn't like CJ so much, I'd just kill the motherfucker and deliver his head to Rezzer on a platter."

"Warlord Rezzer will be most grateful that you do not," Vance said, a small smile turning up the corners of his mouth.

"Yeah? Well, he can owe CJ about a thousand backrubs and two thousand orgasms as payment."

Marz choked at her bold words. Vance laughed. I looked at my warrior mate and smiled. Two thousand orgasms? It might take years, but I was more than up to the task. After all, I could not live knowing an Atlan pleased his mate more than I pleasured mine. I just hadn't had enough time with her. Forever would do.

As if she could read my mind, my female turned to me. "If you really want to do this, then let's go, Mak." She waved a hand absently at Marz and Vance as she walked away. "I'll activate the beacon at the exact coordinates when I'm ready for Rezz and his beast friends to storm the joint."

Marz protested, but Gwen ignored him and I couldn't take my eyes off the sway of her ass, the seductive slide of her long, glossy black hair as it fell down her back as I followed her to the empty Hive ship.

This ship was ours now. And I now understood that Gwen had no intention of ever giving it up. Not until the war was over, or all of the Nexus units were dead. I'd been wrong to think she'd be content on The Colony, going on mission after mission. That having such a small part to play would be enough for her. I'd been so wrong. Looking at her now, she was right. She wanted to go after the Hive, to destroy them, but she wouldn't be able to do it by the governor's rules. She might not strip bare for him to see what she'd been turned into, but the intel she collected and the way she did it alone would make her a weapon to the Coalition.

A *thing,* not a person.

She, too, had to escape. As long as she let me fight next to her, I didn't care what kind of ship we called home. Or what color she was when we went to sleep at night.

"Are you two planning on fighting the Hive naked?" Vance called after us.

"Of course not," Gwen replied easily. "They have S-Gen units on every ship. We'll make our own gear." The spontaneous matter generators were common on every Coalition vessel in the Fleet. Every household had one on the developed worlds. It created everything from weapons and clothing to food and personal items with recycled quantum energy formed into new molecules. If the hive had S-Gen units, we'd want for nothing.

She disappeared up the ship's ramp and I followed, sighing in relief when she closed the door and filled the small room with breathable air.

The moment I was able, I pulled off my helmet and hauled her to me for a kiss.

By the gods, she was magnificent, no matter what color she was.

"Get that damn uniform off and toss it, Mak. They need to think you've been captured. At least for a while."

"Are you telling me to get naked, female?"

"Yes, Mak. I am."

"Good. Then it will be easier to fuck you after I spank you."

11

Gwen, Surface of The Colony Moon, on board the Hive ship

"What?"

"You heard me," he replied.

"You're going to spank me? What for?" The guy was insane if he thought he was going to get his hands on me—at least that way. I was all for the fucking part.

"For putting yourself in danger. For not *listening* to a single thing I said. For taking on *nine* Hive all by yourself."

The way he said the word *nine* had me taking a step back. His face was red, tendons in his neck becoming extended. His fangs were hanging low, just over the edge of his bottom lip. Yeah, he was pissed.

"But I didn't want you to get hurt. It's not like you could listen to them, to know their thoughts. To kill them."

He took a step closer. "You think me weak, mate?"

I shook my head, swallowed. The intensity on his face as he toed off his boots, stripped out of his clothes, made me nervous.

"No. Of course not."

"You did what you thought you must. I can't go back and change it now. But I *can* change your mind about doing something so reckless in the future."

Before I could turn around and run off—not that there was any place for me to really go on the small ship—he had me tossed over his shoulder. His hand came down on my butt as he walked me toward... somewhere. Since I was upside down and staring at his taut, bare ass, I was a little distracted.

Besides, that one swat stung. His hand was huge!

"You will not rush into battle alone, do you understand me, mate? It is my right and my privilege to protect you. I can't do that if you leave me behind."

He dropped me onto a bed and I watched as he put his hands on his hips. He stood like a warrior, all sinewy muscles, strong physique and gorgeous cock. I'd pricked his ego by running off and taking care of the Hive myself. I could do it without him. I *had* done it. Showed him I wasn't weak. But proving it only hurt him. Not only emotionally because he was angry, but deep down in his very DNA. He was hard-wired to protect a female. Cherish her. Keep her safe from harm. Away from lunatics like the Hive. Yet I'd taken that ability from him.

Now, he was gaining his control back. And spanking me would be proof of it, that I was with him, safe and that he once again had control over me.

Like he ever did. But I could let him think so. Let him get himself back in check, on even ground. Knowing I could do this to him was heady, powerful stuff. That I could practically bring him to his knees with emotion was intense.

I put my feet on the bed, spread them wide, let him look his fill. See all of me. "I'm sorry, Mak. But you know I can take care of myself. I proved that today."

"What if there had been fifty Hive? A hundred? What if they had advanced weaponry? No. You do not fight alone. Not anymore." He devoured me with his eyes, his cock straining toward me. Big. Eager. I knew that cock, knew it would stretch me wide and be hard. Rough. Wild. God, I wanted him wild.

"Come here, Mak."

He shook his head, his gaze locked like a laser on my wet pussy lips. "You want your spanking on your pussy?" he asked.

Instantly, I closed my knees. "What? No!"

"Then roll over and present that ass."

I had to admit—to myself, I wasn't going to tell Mak this—his bossiness in the bedroom made me hot. I didn't want my pussy spanked, sheesh, but I did want his dirty talk. And I didn't mind that hot hand on my ass, either.

And so I rolled over and up onto my hands and knees, curved my back so my ass was up and presented to him.

"Ah, mate, I love seeing my handprint all pink and pretty on your ass. Now to add a few more."

He spanked me again and I rocked forward. I hissed at the sting but bent my head down, inspected the weeping tip of his cock through the vee of my legs, the way it jumped at every small sound I made. Testing my power over him, I shifted back, closer to him, making sure he could see the wetness coating my aching pussy. His spanking stung, but it didn't hurt. Not really. Not enough to counteract the thrill I had submitting to him, letting him do what he wanted with me.

All my life had been about fighting. Resisting. First at home, then in the military and Coalition ReCon. Even more when the Hive had caught and tortured me, turned me into what I was now. Arriving on The Colony had offered no relief, for as soon as I appeared, the males began fighting over me. Following me. Trying to seduce me. Win me over. Claim me for their own.

But I'd chosen Mak. I *wanted* his touch, his hands on my body. His mind attuned to my needs. I *needed* him to care. And right now, he trembled with emotions I didn't dare name, even as he spanked my bottom. Made my skin burn and my heart explode with love and lust and trust. I'd never trusted anyone the way I did Makarios of Kronos, the rebel, smuggler, criminal. Because he was *mine*.

"This won't be a full spanking because we don't have time. I want to be balls deep inside you within two minutes. But you will know the feel of my hand, to know what will happen the next time you decide to run off to fight the Hive by yourself."

Another spank landed.

"Got it?"

"Yes, sir," I breathed. The sting was spreading, morphing into something different, something... primordial. A caveman claiming his woman. Well, this wasn't a claiming, but it was going to be a good fucking. I was primed and ready. Needy. No doubt he could see my pussy was wet, practically dripping for him.

"Ah, I like the sound of that obedience."

Looking over my shoulder at him, I could tell he liked it a lot. He wasn't as restrained as I thought. His face was tense, but his gaze heated. Every line of his body screamed power. Even his cock, which stuck straight out from the dark nest of curls, ruddy, hard, pulsing. There was pre-cum slipping from the tip, eager for me.

"Please," I whispered, hoping he'd fuck me. Now.

I needed it. The adrenaline was bleeding away and I needed it. Needed a release, needed to feel real. Human. Alive. I needed Mak.

He stepped up closer to the bed, hooked his right arm about my waist to pull me up so I was lifted completely off my knees. His cock prodded my entrance and he aligned his thighs to mine then thrust up in one hard stroke.

Impaled, I gasped, bucked. He didn't give me time to adjust to his massive size. Just took. Controlled. Dominated. He pushed me away and pulled me to him like I weighed nothing. Fucked me. Filled me. The lower half of my body was in the air and I had no control, no traction, could only take what he gave me.

With a groan, he increased his pace, lifted my shoulders off the bed with his left hand, cupped my breast as he held my back to his chest. My head fell back against his shoulder. When I melted against him, he turned, walking us toward a smooth, cold wall. He pressed my body to the wall and moved both hands to the underside of my thighs, spreading me open, holding me up, fucking me from behind like he'd never get enough.

He fucked me like this, our bodies meshed together. Hard, wild. Rough.

The sound of flesh slapping filled the small room. The scent of fucking lingered in the air. My pussy quivered around him, not being given any time to adjust. My tender bottom was given no reprieve as his hips pressed into it over and over.

"You will come, mate."

The idea of coming just because he commanded it would have been laughable. Before. I could barely come from a guy alone, not without some kind of stimulation of my clit. Especially like this. But I'd been primed, not just from the battle with the Hive, but the battle with Mak for dominance. Power. Control.

I might be powerful outside these walls, but here, now, his cock filling me hard and deep, unrelenting, filling me with his seed, he held the power. The harsh growl as he climaxed proved it.

And I was willing to give myself to him. Eager to surrender control, to stop fighting. Whatever he wanted to give me, I'd take. Whatever he asked, I'd give. Everything. And so I came. My scream bounced off the walls and loosened something in me, in my heart.

God, I wanted Mak. Forever. Even if it meant submitting to him. Because in the end, I was the one who received the greatest gift.

I forgot everything but him. The Hive, the governor, The Colony. Nexus 4 and even my blueness, the torture and pain. The war. I forgot everything outside the room because all that mattered was Mak.

Gwen, Hive Ship, Integration Chamber

"COME HERE, MAK." I grabbed his hand and pulled him

through the door into what passed as a mini Hive medical station.

The Coalition called them Integration Stations because these were the rooms where newly acquired biological specimens were fitted with new Hive integrations. A very diplomatic term for what the Coalition worlds considered torture chambers, the Hive who lived and worked on these ships considered their doctors and medical stations.

He stalled just outside the doorway. "I'm not going in there."

"Yes, you are. I have a plan."

He allowed me to pull him into the room without a fight, for which I was grateful. "This is *our* new medical unit, on *our* new ship, so you'd better get used to it."

"I will use it when necessary," he replied, his tone grim. "Other than that, I will never set foot in this room."

"Fine." I let him go and rummaged through several storage spaces until I found what I was looking for. With a happy smile, I walked back to my mate and held up the small glass specimen tube. "Bite the top of this."

"What?"

"Bite into this. Stick one of those fangs through the seal and get some venom in there. I want to analyze it." He took a step back from me, shaking his head. God, he was huge. And sexy. And so fucking hot I wanted to tear that armor off him and jump him again.

Thanks to the onboard S-Gen unit, we were both fully dressed in newly generated battle armor. His, a dark black and brown camouflage pattern that matched the rest of the Coalition Fleet. Me? I was dressed in armor as well, but it was a deep, striking blue, the patterns designed to match the exact flow of colors on my Hive skin. Mak didn't want me going into battle again without armor, and this way, I could still tempt the Nexus with *exactly* what was underneath. If he just skimmed me with those creepy dark eyes, he might not even notice that the blue curves were armored, and not natural flesh.

But then, what was natural to a monster?

"Gwen, my bite is deadly. There is no reason for me to do this."

"Humor me." I walked to him slowly and melted into his body, pressing my lips to the center of his chest because as tall as I was, that was all I could reach when he was wearing his boots. "Please? Pretty, pretty please with a cherry on top?"

His entire body shuddered and I knew I'd won. "I don't know what a cherry is, but I'll take some pussy on top later as payment instead."

Laughing, I lifted the specimen tube to his mouth, trying not to show how much his dirty words affected me. "I'll go cowgirl on you anytime you want, Mak."

He grabbed my wrist as I was about to stab his fang into the end of the tube. "What is cowgirl?"

I grinned at him and made sure he could feel my free hand exploring the stone hard muscles of his ass. "You lay down on your back and I ride your cock."

"Like that first time?"

"Yes."

A growl rumbled from his chest. "Yes. As soon as we're done with this mission."

"I agree with that."

"I will also require you to be cowgirl on my lips, mate. I will taste you again before you come, and I will do it with you straddling my face."

"Deal." As if I'd ever say no to having his wicked lips and tongue working on me.

I shoved his fang into the vial and waited a few seconds for the vacuum tube to do its job and the venom to drip into the bottom. When I had several drops of the pearly liquid, I pulled it away from him and swatted his ass as hard as I dared, then scampered out of reach to the analysis station. Loading his venom into one of the small ports, I found myself humming. Happy. About to go into battle with an evil that had been at war with the Coalition for centuries… and I was happy.

The data was immediate, the display clearly stating what Mak had said. His venom was poisonous. But, it also asked if I wished an antidote to be made and I quickly pushed the button for yes.

The ship could work on an antidote while we took care of a few small problems on the planet's surface. And then? I'd take a dose, climb on his cock for that cowgirl ride and shove Mak's fangs into my shoulder myself if I had to. He was *mine*. If he wasn't leaving me, wasn't heading home to Rogue 5 and Kronos, then he was going to claim me properly.

End. Of. Discussion.

Mak watched me, arms crossed, clearly not amused. But he didn't try to stop me. That was one of the things I loved about him. He let me be me.

Once the machine was doing its thing, I turned to him with a smile, ran and jumped into his arms. He caught me, of course. I knew he would.

"Kiss me, Mak. Kiss me, and then let's go kill monsters."

"Whatever makes you happy, female."

I smiled at him, stroked my hand down his rugged cheek. "You, Mak. You make me happy."

He froze, staring into my eyes as if I'd shocked him. Before I could go all misty eyed, or start spouting *I love you* or other silly nonsense, I kissed him. Hard. Fast. With everything, telling him without words how much he meant to me. Because the truth was, I wasn't sure I could beat Nexus 4. The Nexus units were powerful. Tricky. Evil. Completely without conscience or morals. Their minds were so strong, it had been a freaking miracle I'd escaped the first time. And now I was going back for more. Voluntarily.

But I was going to try. I was stronger now. A lot stronger. Plus, I had Mak.

I pulled back and turned away, heading for the cockpit and the co-pilot's seat before he could say anything. I was a good pilot, but he was exceptional, and I wasn't so proud that I couldn't admit he was far better than I.

"Gwen." His voice called to me, but I didn't stop or turn around.

"Come on, Mak. We've only got fifteen minutes to get down there." I didn't want to hear words of love or devotion or the word *mate* right now. I needed to go into this battle with nothing to lose. I needed to focus my entire being on defeating Nexus 4.

I needed to protect Makarios.

12

Gwen, Hive Ship, The Colony, Cave Entrance North of Base 3

I LEANED over the instrument panel and placed my palm flat on the screen. Odd thing, being part machine. I could talk to the Hive ship without *talking*. It read my mind, which was just freaky, but came in very, very handy.

The first thing I'd done when I turned the baby on was reprogram the ship's security protocols to the highest level. No one but me, Mak, or a Nexus unit could change any security setting on the ship. And to do that, the Nexus would have to be physically present. The ship was ours, mine and Mak's, unless a Nexus unit happened to saunter on board and take control. I felt like I was on the Millennium Falcon and I was Han Solo. But that meant that Mak was Chewbacca, and while he was big enough, that was where the comparisons ended.

Maybe Mak was Han Solo and I'd be Princess Leia. And the Nexus were like Darth Vader.

Yeah, not quite. But no Nexus were getting on this ship. No fucking way.

If that happened, we'd screwed up somewhere along the way and we'd be fucked at that point anyway, so I didn't worry about it. So long as no lower ranking Hive, pirate, smuggler, or Coalition warrior could steal our ship, that was good enough for me. And with the new settings, the ship wouldn't even start for anyone else. No power. No navigation. Nothing.

"Okay, Mak, this baby is all ours." I told him what I'd done as I rubbed my hands together. The Hive ship was small, meant to hold a group of no more than eighteen for extended periods of time. But that meant for just the two of us, she was massive. Three sleeping chambers, a full S-Gen unit with seating for eight in a dining room. Since the Hive probably worked on three rotations, it meant one third of them would eat at any given time. The Hive were nothing if not mechanized. "Our baby needs a name."

My voice cracked on the word *baby* and I wanted to slap myself for being so stupid. Mak noticed. *Of course,* he fucking noticed.

"What is wrong, mate? Why are you upset?"

Okay. In for a penny, in for a pound, right? "I don't know why I'm thinking about this now, but I don't know if I can have children, Mak. I don't know if you want that, but I don't know if I can. Or even if I want to. I can't promise you babies. I can't give you that. I just can't..."

He put his hand on top of mine. "I want you, female. I will fight for you, die for you, kill for you. Should you choose to have children, I will do the same for them because they are yours and mine. If not, I am perfectly content spanking your ass for your silly thoughts for the rest of our lives. I do not need children to be happy."

"Okay then." He spoke as if he were giving a lecture in a history class. Facts. Emotionless. True. And just like that I could breathe again. Why I had to tell him about babies now, I had no idea, but I felt better. "Okay. Let's do this."

Leaning over, I pressed the locator beacon that would signal Rezzer and the other Atlans to join us. We'd landed easily on The Colony's surface, cleared by the governor so we weren't shot to Kingdom Come. We were just waiting for the others and we'd get this show on the road. Get shit done and finally, and forever, get off this planet.

As soon as the beacon pinged, I placed my hand on the ship's control panel and made contact with Captain Marz's private comm line. His face filled the small screen before me and I marveled at how similar Hive technology was to that of the Coalition. Degrees of separation.

"Marz, can you hear me?"

"Yes. I have Maxim and Ryston with me as well."

Marz stepped aside and the governor's face filled the small screen.

"Governor."

"No. I am Maxim Rone. First Mate to Rachel and we demand justice for the traitor Krael. I am not the governor right now, Gwen. This conversation never happened."

I nodded once. "Good. Then the Intelligence Core will never know that you gave me Coalition flight codes in exchange for information on the location of the Prillon traitor Krael Gerton and a Hive shipment of transport mineral scheduled to depart your planet in less than an hour."

The governor—no, Maxim—growled at me, his eyes almost glowing with his irritation. "You are a very difficult female."

"And we both know you are going to give me the codes. I need to be able to travel through Coalition space without fear of being attacked. I can get to the other Nexus units, Maxim. You give me the codes, I give you the information you need to save The Colony, the transport system, keep us in the war and give you the vengeance you crave for Krael's attempt on your life. It's a win-win."

Behind him, I heard another male voice, less controlled. More rage.

Ryston.

"Do it. Let her hunt the bastards. Let's take care of our own. Think of Rachel and our son." Their baby boy was beautiful, and only a few months old. And both warriors turned to jelly the moment the little one was placed in their hands.

Maxim's eyes narrowed and he nodded to someone off screen. Moments later, at least a dozen flight codes arrived in our ship's database, and in my head. They were too precious to leave behind. These codes would get me through Coalition controlled space without incident. The Hive codes buried in the ship would get me deep into Hive territory, if needed. And I had to believe that with Mak's connections on Rogue 5, we could get anything else we needed to slip in and out of star systems like a ghost ship.

"Thank you, Maxim. And good hunting." I signed off, simultaneously sending him the exact coordinates and layout of the mines where the Hive transport ship was located. I included guard counts and Hive Soldier locations as well as the countdown until takeoff with the stolen minerals.

He had less than an hour to take care of his tasks, but I had confidence he'd figure things out.

Nodding to Mak, I watched him shut down the ship to stand-by mode and we both grabbed our weapons, left our Millennium Falcon behind and headed for the cave.

Five minutes later, we walked to the entrance of the cave system to find not just Warlord Rezzer, but Braun, Tane, the Everian Hunter, Kiel, the silver eyed human, Denzel, and another massive Warlord I'd never seen before. He was as big as Mak, and he wasn't even in beast mode.

I looked him up and down, to which he smiled.

"I am Warlord Bryck, governor of Base 2."

My eyebrows shot up at that information. "Base 2? Then why are you here?"

"I am here because Krael murdered a good man, Captain Brooks, from Earth. He polluted our entire planet with Quell, a chemical that steals our minds. I am here for vengeance for all the warriors lost to his treachery."

Okay. Hard core. "You're in the wrong place. Krael is miles from here, in another cave. I can give you the coordinates, if you want. You might be able to transport there in time for the battle."

"Who goes to the fight?"

I looked at Mak, not sure what I should or shouldn't say. If Maxim wasn't acting as the governor right now, would he want anyone to know he was in that cave? Another governor? I wasn't sure how the politics worked. Mak was male, a warrior, and he'd been here longer than I had. I lot longer.

"Maxim and Ryston seek vengeance for the traitor's assassination attempt, as well as his long ago attack on their mate," Mak said. "The other Prillon warriors accompany them to eliminate Krael."

The huge Atlan governor looked from Mak back to me. "This is your operation?"

"Yes."

"Then I request permission to remain here with my Atlan brothers. I have faith that the Prillon warriors will see Krael dead."

I had no doubt about that myself. "Okay. Let's do this." I turned to the six warriors, plus Mak. I'd never had this much backup before. Holy shit. They were all huge, and Rezzer was half in beast mode already, his face elongated, eager to kill Nexus 4. But a full frontal assault wouldn't work. Not this time. "I'm going in. Give me exactly two minutes, and then come in with everything you've got."

"No." Mak spoke before the others had the chance.

I turned to face Mak. "I have to get close, hurt him before you get there or he'll kill every single one of you. He's strong, Mak. Stronger than me. We can't overpower him."

"How many Hive does he have with him?" The Everian Hunter, Kiel, asked, the calculating gleam behind his eyes betraying not a hint of nerves or fear. I'd heard he could run so fast, move so quickly, that he was impossible to track with the naked eye.

I'd like to see that.

"The last information I had said twelve. But that could be more or less, as they've had two hours to adapt."

"He knows you're coming?" Bryck asked.

"Yes. He does. And since I killed nine of his Soldiers up on the moon's surface, he's not too happy with me either."

"What?" Braun looked at Mak, as if the death toll was his fault.

Mak arched a brow and looked down at me as if to say, *See? I'm not the only one. You deserved that spanking, reckless female.*

"Forget about that." I waved my hand in the air as if killing nine Hive was inconsequential. "The Nexus unit is blue. Dark blue. Like this." In front of all of them, I changed so my face, neck and hands which showed my only visible skin turned blue to match my armor, knowing it would tip off Nexus 4 that I was close. But I needed them to see and to understand. "Look at me," I ordered Braun.

He did. He stared into my eyes and I used the telepathic power the Hive had given me to hold him in my mind, trap him there, just for a few seconds, to make him want to stay. When I let him go, he lurched backward with a curse.

"Shit," he muttered, shaking his head, as if that would help erase what had just happened.

"Look into his eyes, and he'll own you. You'll kill your own mates for him without hesitation and believe it is right. Now at least you know more about your opponent. This is no simple Hive drone. So after the two minutes, follow me in and kill anything that moves, but leave the Nexus to me and Mak. And whatever happens, do not look into its eyes."

The males were all staring at me, at my blue face, black hair, shark eyes. I knew exactly what I looked like. A nightmare. No, a *monster* from their worst nightmares.

Braun stepped forward and stared at me for long seconds before dropping to take a knee, bowing before me as the Hive had done. "You are the bravest warrior I have ever known, Gwendolyn of Earth. You are an honorable female. I pledge my life to your protection."

"No, I don't—" I didn't get to finish the sentence. All of them, even Mak, had taken a knee.

He looked up at me. "Command us, mate. We are yours."

I was stunned. Confused. Honored.

Taking a deep breath, I accepted their salute and tried not to let it make my heart hurt. Which was impossible. Especially with Mak and his big, brown eyes staring up at me like I was the sun and the stars, his everything. "Okay. I'm going in. Give me two minutes. Two *full* minutes. Then come in fighting."

Unable to stop myself, I leaned down and kissed Mak on the lips. "Stay alive." It was an order. If he got killed, I'd chase him into the afterlife and kill him again.

Before he could argue, I was gone, using my Nexus speed to run through the cave faster than any human, or beast, or even Everian Hunter. Although I'd never been in a footrace with Kiel of Everis, I was confident I could take him.

No mere mortal could see me, not moving at full speed. I wasn't a blur; I was a blast of wind. Gone before anyone realized I'd passed by.

But the Hive weren't human. Not anymore. Their implants tracked me as I sped by, but none tried to stop me.

I was Nexus. Summoned by Nexus 4. Expected.

One of them.

I could hear the buzz of excitement building in the cave with my arrival. Even though they were Hive, underneath it all they were still emotional creatures. They still experienced the effects of fear, adrenaline, anxiety.

I could hear them in my head talking to me, about me, but I ignored them all. I did smile when I was reminded of Nexus 4's anger with me over the loss of their Soldiers on the moon, but I ignored even that, heading for the center of the noise in my head, the silent black hole at the eye of the storm. Nexus 4 broadcast nothing. He was a dead zone, a darkness so deep and dark that falling into his mind was like tumbling through an ink black well with no bottom. It went on forever, with no way out. No walls. Nothing one could use for reference. Nothing but *him*.

And his mind was cold. So, so cold.

That cold embraced me now and my entire body responded out of reflex, the massive number of Hive implants and microcellular integrations resonating to his call. My body was a guitar string and he'd just played an entire chord. The Hive parts of me, and there were a lot of them, hummed, charged on Nexus energy. *Alive*.

It felt like a million tiny spiders crawling around on the underside of my skin. My skin didn't crawl... the cells beneath my skin did. Slid around. Moved and reorganized themselves into a likeness of him, instead of Nexus 2.

They were vain, the Nexus. Nexus 4 would not want a female who looked like his rival, the one who had made me, Nexus 2.

I stopped on a dime, less than three steps from him. But not because I wanted to stop. No. He forced me, took control of all the little parts and pieces inside me that were *his*.

And I hated him for moving me like a puppet master moved a marionette. Hated him with a passion and vehemence I never could have managed before Mak. Before I knew what a violation this monster's influence truly was. What it was to be loved by a mate, to be free and wanted for being myself. What *goodness* was.

Still, I had a role to play. I didn't try to hide the hate. My ire had amused Nexus 2, made him feel more powerful. I counted on the fact that Nexus 4 was no different.

"Where is Nexus 2?" His voice was deep, hypnotic, and

the words flowed to my ears and directly into my mind as one. I stared at his feet, not daring to raise my gaze, not even to his waist or his chest. It was just too dangerous.

Instantly, without thinking, I offered him the truth. "I don't know. I left him behind."

His laugh was more hiss than chuckle. If a cobra could laugh, I imagined it would sound like him. "No longer playing games, are we. Not *we* don't know?"

"I left Nexus 2. He is weak. Vain. I came here, looking for you. I had hoped you would be more powerful than Nexus 2. Not so easy to defeat. But I have lost hope. Your Soldiers were easy to find. Even easier to kill."

He stepped toward me and I fought his desire to have me kneel. My fight lasted for only a fraction of a second as he felt the resistance and pushed harder. I landed on my knees so hard I would have cracked my kneecap if I'd still been human.

"I am not amused by your challenge, female. Those were my Soldiers. My assets. You will repay me tenfold."

"Only if I stay."

He was close now, so close my nose was inches from his thigh, his large blue hand right there so I could see the vile black liquid pumping through its veins. I couldn't think of him as a man. I just couldn't. Not anymore.

When his hand moved toward my throat, I struck. Hard. Fast. With every ounce of strength I possessed. The blade hidden up my sleeve springing forward into my palm less than a second before I shoved the silver into his torso.

But he was faster. He dodged the strike so that my dagger missed his heart by several inches.

Fuck. Fuck. Fuck.

Had it been two minutes yet?

Where was Mak? How long would it take him to get here?

Nexus 4 ignored the blade protruding from his abdomen like I'd stuck him with a toothpick. His hand wrapped around my neck and he lifted me by my jaw, walking toward the side of the cave until he held me pinned there. His control of my body was complete. I couldn't fight. Couldn't kick. Hit.

But I could close my eyes. And I did. Hard. He could kill me, but he wouldn't own me. Not again.

"I feel your fear, female. There is no need for such a useless emotion. It cripples you." His voice was soothing. Calm. So very, very safe.

I fought against the feeling. "Fuck you."

"Do you think the Atlan warriors charging through the cave will save you?"

I said nothing. His hissing laughter made me want to scream, so I did. The sound echoed through the cave, bouncing off the rock walls, the wail of a wounded animal, of terror and rage and a fight to the death.

"Very well. Now you have made the Hyperion angry. Hmm, not just Hyperion. Something more. Interesting and rare. I had hoped not to kill him. I have an accord with Cerberus, but some things can't be helped."

"You're a sociopath."

"I am efficient, human. And soon, you will be as well."

I heard the other Hive Soldiers step in close, one on each side of me. I was not surprised when they pried open my eyelids. I tried to fight, but Nexus 4 held me as easily as holding a block of wood in place. I couldn't move.

This plan was fucked, and if I lived through this, Mak

and I would have to seriously rethink our strategy for taking down the rest of them.

"You think you can hunt us all? My, my, what an ambitious little female." The Hive on either side of me held open my eyelids and Nexus 4 stepped closer. "What merciless children you will breed."

He sounded pleased. And drowning in his gaze, in the loneliness and stark need I saw there, I started to feel pleased as well. Nexus 4 needed me. Would always protect me. He was alone, and only I could please him, make him whole.

I was confused and could barely breathe. No. Mak. He needed me, too. Makarios. I needed him. He needed me. This was wrong. Nexus 4 was in my mind.

Mak's roar of rage echoed through the cavern as the Nexus hissed at me. "Nexus 2 made you too strong. A critical miscalculation. You will be eliminated."

"Fuck you."

He squeezed until I saw stars, but his focus had shifted. I had my legs back under my own control once again so I used them. I kicked him in the knees, the thighs, anywhere I could reach. Grabbing blindly for the knife in his abdomen, I found it. Twisted. Pushed deeper. Tried to move it up where I wanted it to go. To end him.

Mak

THE NEXUS UNIT had my mate up against the wall, his hand around her neck as two Hive Soldiers pried open her eyes.

I knew the moment she was lost. Her body, rigid before, went limp, as if she relaxed in his arms. Under his control.

Fuck no.

The roar escaped me in challenge. I was going to kill that creature. Rip his head from his shoulders. Tear him limb from limb. Pound his body into a pool of entrails and jelly.

All around me, the Atlans were in beast mode as they tore the Hive Soldiers into pieces. Ripped off their arms and legs. Broke necks and threw bodies against the walls. I'd fought my share, was covered in blood from head to toe. But I ignored the fighting around me, focused on one thing. My mate.

Gwen.

Mine.

And he was hurting her. Told her she was too strong, that he would eliminate her.

"Fuck you." Her defiance was music to my ears. She was still in there, fighting.

I ran as she kicked. I heard her cry of rage as she reached for the knife I could now see protruding from his chest.

It hurt him, but it wasn't enough to take him out. He would kill her.

"Mine!" The word was howled by the Hyperion beast, not me. I didn't grow taller or wider, as the Atlans did. But my fangs were down, claws came out, longer and sharper than anything I knew I was capable of. They were thick, like blades, and razor sharp, dripping in the venom special to my kind. One swipe, and the bastard would bleed to death. They'd never appeared before, but then I'd never had a mate in mortal danger.

I'd use them on him if I didn't tear out his throat with my teeth first.

The Nexus must have realized the true danger was behind him, for he dropped Gwen to the ground and turned to me with a snarl of his own.

Gwen warned me not to look in his eyes, but there was nothing living that could tear a Hyperion beast from his mate. Nothing.

I stared the blue creature in the eye, challenge in every line of my body, in my snarl. I stared into the black depths and felt... nothing but rage. And an urge to kill.

"Gwen is mine." The beast spoke but the male in me agreed. Mine.

"I'd rather not kill you," Nexus 4 said. "I do not wish to break the accord I have with Rogue 5."

I raked my claws through the air. "Lies. I will slash your blue throat."

Behind him, Gwen pushed to her feet and looked up at me. I saw the movement out of the corner of my eye, but I didn't dare take my eyes off the real threat, the Nexus in front of me. He was big, almost as big as me. Dark blue from head to toe. On him it looked natural. The only truly odd thing about him was a large arc of tissue that ran from the base of his skull down his back in large branches like a tree.

If I had to guess, I'd bet that was where his mind control organs were. Which meant I wanted to crush them.

"He made a deal with Cerberus," Gwen told me. "He said so earlier."

"Cerberus does not speak for Rogue 5." My words were dark, lethal as I met the bastard's gaze head on.

"Are you a member of Cerberus legion?"

"Never."

"Then I can kill you without consequence."

He moved like lightning, aiming for my head. Instinct saved me. I put my hands up, the claws finding his chest as I shoved him away and to the side. He regained his balance instantly and we circled one another. I stared him in the eye the entire time.

"Look out!" Gwen screamed, her indrawn breath warning me that the Nexus was about to move. Not that I didn't know.

Catching him in my claws once more, I lowered my mouth to his shoulder and bit deep, ripping with every bit of strength I possessed. Yanking hard, I pulled a piece of his shoulder from his body as he screamed in pain. The sound was music to my ears. The taste of his blood driving my beast to a frenzy. Blood. It was just blood. Black as night but blood just like a billion others.

The Nexus twisted in an attempt to escape from my claws, but they were deep, and I was not letting him go.

Unable to free himself, he wrapped his legs around me and squeezed. Ribs cracked. Pain lanced sharp and hot. I couldn't breathe.

I refused to let go.

"Mak!"

I heard Gwen's cry, but didn't see her moving until she was on the Nexus's back, pulling at the odd curved appendage there.

The Nexus screamed as something inside it cracked and popped, the sound of breaking clear but it could have been metal or bone. I had no idea which.

With a warrior's cry, Gwen ripped the organ completely free and threw it across the room. She leaped off the Nexus's back and I dug my claws in deeper, until I could feel the beat of his heart against my fingertips. I pushed the creature down onto its knees, as he'd done to my mate, and looked up into her eyes, a question shimmering in my own gaze.

She looked at me, then slowly shook her head.

"He is for Rezzer."

Yes. Rezzer. This thing had tried to kill the Atlan's mate, destroy their unborn twins, murder his mate and family. The Atlan deserved justice.

"Rezzer." I shouted his name but I needn't have. He stood less than three steps away, waiting.

His beast was out in full force. Covered in blood from head to toe, he looked like he'd just stepped off the battlefield. But then again, he had. We all had.

Gwen looked at Rezzer, then Braun, who was back in his true Atlan form, capable of speaking in complete sentences. "Are they all dead?"

"Dead." The deep rumble was Rezzer as he paced next to Nexus 4, savoring the moment.

Braun cleared his throat. "I heard from Maxim. Their mission is complete. They were successful. Every single one of them is dead. Here and there. It's over."

"Good." Gwen walked to my side and placed her hand on my shoulder. Her grin was almost evil. She patted me then and her smile was just for me. "Let Rezzer have him and let's go. You and I are done. I need a shower."

And a fucking spanking. Then she'd sit on my face and I'd make her come until she passed out.

The thought of my mate naked made the decision a quick one. In seconds, the newly discovered claws retracted and I shoved the bleeding Nexus unit in Rezzer's general direction.

I didn't look back. Didn't want to see what the Atlans did

to him. Didn't care. Whatever torture they could come up with was more than deserved.

Somehow, I didn't think it would last long. Rezzer was in no mood to play with the thing. He wanted to kill. Just as I had when I saw the enemy with a hand around my mate's throat.

She slid her blood covered hand into mine, and I held it like the precious gift it was. The blood would wash away, but she was mine. The affection I saw shining from her eyes was mine. And if I had time to give her two thousand orgasms, perhaps that affection would grow to love.

I wanted her to love me. Not just need my body or physical release. She'd seen the darkness in me now, knew about my bite. And she wasn't running, but leading me back to our ship.

When she wrapped her hand around my arm and asked me to carry her, my heart soared. I lifted her in my arms and held her close to my heart. "Always, mate. It is my pleasure to hold you."

She sighed and snuggled against me. "Who knew you'd turn out to be such a sweet-talker?"

13

Mak, Open Space

I WAS IN OPEN SPACE. Fuck, yes. With the never-ending blackness out the cockpit window, I finally felt free. No sectors, no battlegroups. Just unclaimed, uncharted universe. It was a familiar sensation, this need to be in control of my life, my destiny, but it has been some time. So much had happened since I'd been set up, since the traitor I now knew came from Cerberus, had destroyed everything I'd built. Ruined me. Led to my capture, first by the Coalition, then my capture and torture by the Hive. The struggle for survival. Escape. The unending days sentenced to a prisoner's life on The Colony. It had all been his fault.

And now, I had to thank the traitor for my mate. For Gwen. And every dark thing I'd survived, every agony, the rage. It was all worth it.

I had planned to hunt the traitor, return to Rogue 5 and

have my revenge. Now I was content alerting Kronos to the problem and letting the legion deal with it. I had more important things to do. Like keep my mate alive.

Glancing at the co-pilot's seat beside me, I realized that my destiny wasn't as I'd thought. No, my life was with Gwen. I studied her as she stared out into the vast emptiness, the look of awe, of all-encompassing peace on her face. With her long hair pulled back, her cheeks smeared with dust and blood from the cave, her body armor covered in dirt, gore and tearstains on the dark blue clothing, she'd never looked more beautiful.

And she was mine completely. Well, almost. Except for the lack of official claiming, I had her body and soul.

And she me in return. I would want no other. I needed her, my other half, the other half of my soul. I was a Forsian poet in my thoughts, but they couldn't be helped.

As the governor had said, he was pussy whipped. An Earth term his mate Rachel had told him about, I remembered him laughing. He was completely under his mate's power. Weaker, smaller and somewhat helpless on The Colony without a protector, she had all the control of her two Prillon mates.

It was the same for Gwen. She had all the control. I could deny her nothing. Yet she wasn't weak of body. She was strong. Too strong. She didn't need me to survive, to keep her safe. She was self-sufficient and yet she wanted me beside her on this adventure to... who the fuck knew?

"What?" she asked, catching me looking at her.

I smiled. Really smiled. "Nothing. We have the entire universe to explore. Together."

She pursed her lips.

"What?" I asked in return.

"Do you know how to turn on the auto pilot on this thing?" She looked at the displays that filled the snug cabin.

"Of course."

"While I want to go see the entire universe, I don't need to do it right now."

I arched a brow. "What did you have in mind?"

My cock stirred at the idea of having her climb in my lap and take my cock for a ride. I'd yet to fuck her in every room—every surface of this ship, but it was something I would definitely enjoy from now on.

I undid the harness about my shoulders, the clasp on my chest coming undone beneath my deft fingers. The straps fell to the sides. "I'm all yours."

And I meant it.

She smiled and I could have sworn the sun came out from around the forty-seventh asteroid belt. Undoing her harness, she stood, held out her hand. "Come on."

I frowned. "But don't you want to—"

She took hold of my wrist, tugged me up, pulled me behind her, out of the cockpit and down the central corridor. Only when we were in the central room did she stop. "Oh, I want to. But fucking isn't enough for me. I took the antidote the analysis unit made for me."

"What?" My cock was already hard in my pants, my balls aching to fill her pussy up again. It had been too long since I'd been inside her.

"I don't satisfy you? If you want me on my knees, my mouth on your pussy, it is no hardship. You do not need to be shy about telling me your needs."

She flushed prettily—even after all we'd done together—and shook her head.

"You don't like me eating that sweet pussy?"

She laughed, covered her face with her hand. "It's not that. Yes, of course you satisfy me. You know that well enough, Mr. Big Ego. I love that and you can eat me out all you want."

"Then what is it? I will pleasure you any way you wish."

"Then claim me."

Those three words had the eagerness to fuck slip from me. Like a cold shower tube, I was doused in reality. "I will give you anything but that." I sliced my hand through the air. "I'm not willing to risk your life."

"I told you, I took the antidote. I'm fine."

Antidote. Yes, she had said something about an antidote, but I hadn't heard anything other than I wasn't giving her all she needed. Now, watching as she crossed her arms over her chest, I tried not to notice the way her breasts lifted, even under the layer of armor. Fuck, I loved those breasts, but I needed to focus on what she'd said.

"When did you take this... antidote?"

"I'd forgotten about it after the battle, but got it first thing once back on board. Like I said, I want more, mate."

"We don't know if the antidote is effective or not. It's a Hive med room that's giving us the answers, the fucking antidote, and I don't trust it." She was too precious to me to risk. I'd been able to fuck her fine without my fangs. The pleasure we could share for the rest of our lives without it would be more than fine with me.

"Don't you want to claim me?" she asked. Her eyes were filled with doubt and I hated that.

Closing the distance between us in two strides, I cupped her face in my big palm. "With my very being." My fangs dropped as I said the words, bodily proof of my desire to make her completely and finally mine in every way.

"Then bite me."

I took a step back. "No. It is too dangerous."

She laughed, although it was filled with sadness. I hated that I made her feel this way, but I'd rather her fight with me than be dead.

"Why? You think me *weak?*" Her hands moved to her hips. Fortunately, her doubt was replaced with anger. I never wished her to doubt her perfection.

"I—"

"Who tossed Prillons around in the pit like they were dolls?"

"You," I admitted, remembering how I'd sat in the stands and watched her destroy every male who got near her.

"Who single-handedly destroyed nine Hive soldiers before you or my other babysitters could arrive?"

"The Nexus unit nearly killed you." I glanced down at her arm, to the hole in her pants, the edges of the material torn and singed. She'd fought in that cave, fought for her life, and I was proud of her. But I wouldn't cause her harm.

"I walked freely on the moon, breathing the acidic fog, my lungs healing faster than the acid could destroy them."

"Still—" She was right. Logically, I knew she spoke the truth. But my protective instincts refused to risk her.

She peeled off her uniform, baring her shoulders, giving me a tempting glimpse of her pale flesh. No blood, no wounds. Perfectly whole.

Groaning, I couldn't tear my gaze from her soft skin, the scent of her filling my head and my cock with a rush of blood.

She lifted her hand, pushed at my chest. I was knocked back a step, reminded of her strength. "I'm not weak. I'm not fragile. You won't kill me because as soon as you bite me, I will heal. No bleeding out. No death."

"It's poison!" I shouted, raking my fingers through my hair. I grabbed her by the biceps, lifted her up so we were eye to eye. Our breaths mingled and her gaze met and held mine. "I'm poison to you."

I felt her fumble around, digging for something buried in her pants pocket.

"You're not. I can prove it." She lifted an injector up so I could see it, raising up the lower half of her arm since I had her pinned.

"What is that?" I asked.

"Proof." She dropped the injector to her thigh and I heard the *whoomph* of air that accompanied an injection. "I used the leftover serum to manufacture a larger dose."

I dropped her, stunned. "What?"

"I injected at least three times what your bite would push into my system."

Dropping to my knees, I grabbed her thigh, tugged at the pants she wore and ripped them. "No! Fuck, no. God, Gwen. What have you done?"

I grabbed the injector from her hand, threw it across the room where it clattered, making Gwen startle.

My hands slid over her toned flesh, the firm muscles, the silvery integrations. Being captured and tortured by the Hive was easier than this. It was as if she'd ripped my heart out, held it in the palm of her hand. Then dropped it and stomped on it. I couldn't watch her die. Not now, not after all we'd been through. *Not ever.*

Her hands slid into my hair, stroked and tried to soothe me. "It's fine. I'm fine."

Glancing up at her, I snarled. "No! It's *not* fine! Fuck, woman, you are going to die. The serum is—"

"—destroyed."

I couldn't catch my breath, the panic I felt real. Intense.

"Mak. *Mak.* MAK!" Gwen kept saying my name, but it was only when she took hold of my hand, gripped a finger and bent it backward did I respond.

"Fuck!" I shouted, and she released me immediately.

"The serum has no effect on me because of the antidote and also because, I assume, I heal quickly, thanks to the Hive. There's no time for it to enter the bloodstream and damage me. I'm not going to die. I'm not *normal,* Mak. I'm not human. Not anymore."

I took a breath, then another. She showed no signs of any damage. No difficulty breathing, no blue lips. No seizure. No blood in her eyes. No stopping heart.

Her words were finally processing. The injection had no effect on her. No change. Nothing. She was right.

I ran my hand over my face. "Holy fuck, Gwen. Your heart may not have stopped, but I swear mine just did."

She smiled. "So you can claim me now."

"Claim you now?" I was still on my knees before her. I stripped her and she let me. When I had her naked, I stood, putting my shoulder into her belly as I tossed her over it, carrying her out of the main room and to one of the sleeping quarters. "I'm going to spank your ass now."

"What?" she screeched as I tossed her on the big bed.

Oh yes. My female, whole and with me alone on our own spacecraft. With nothing but time. And no reason not to fully claim her. I could sink my teeth into her shoulder as I filled her with my seed. And the mating cock... it would—

Oh. I hadn't told her about that yet.

I grinned, remembering how surprised she'd been with my aroused cock, and that had been when it was *normal* sized. Yeah, a spanking first, and then I'd share the rest. Hells, I'd show her.

Then I'd fuck her with it.

She was on her back, one knee bent. She was naked, some of her hair having come loose from the tie at her nape. "Why are you going to spank me?"

I reached out, took hold of her ankle and rolled her onto her stomach. "Besides you liking it?"

She sputtered but didn't say anything.

"Because you put yourself in danger with that injector. You will not take chances with your health."

"But I knew it was safe!"

"You knew no such thing." I gritted my teeth, not wanting to think the worst.

"But I'm fine and now you can fuck me and bite me. Claim me, Mak."

I closed my eyes at the sound of those words. *Claim me, Mak.*

How I'd longed to hear those from her lips, especially now when I could actually do it. When I didn't have to deny either of us what we so desperately wanted.

She tugged against my hold on her ankle, but both of us weren't using our full strength. The metal walls in the small room would be dented and destroyed if we really wanted to fight it out. But I sensed she wanted me to know she wasn't going to be completely compliant in this... or anything. I grinned, reaching up with my other hand and grabbed her waist, her back toward me so she was on her hands and knees.

Her glorious heart-shaped ass was there, just waiting for

my mark. I spanked her, the loud crack of it reverberating. She gasped, but it wasn't hard at all. Still, my handprint instantly bloomed on her skin.

"Mak!" she cried, looking over her shoulder and glaring at me. While she looked none too pleased at being spanked, she wiggled her hips and there was heat in her eyes. Unmistakable need there, and making the soft lips of her pussy glisten with welcome.

"You want me to claim you. I am." I lifted my chin. "I like seeing my handprint on you."

"I want more than your hand," she said, pouting, arching her back and thrusting her ass closer to me. "God, I... the serum might not harm me, but it makes me hot. Hot for you. Horny."

My brow arched as I let go of her ankle. She wasn't going to move now. No, she was needy. Eager. I understood that, my fangs dropping not only when I was riled, but when I was desperate to fuck.

Like now.

"Now you know how I feel," I countered. I spanked her again, lightly.

She moaned, then gave me an order I could not refuse. "Strip, mate."

Hastily, I shucked shirt, shoes, socks, everything except my pants. When I was done, she was on her knees facing me. Even with her on the bed, I was taller.

"Need help?" she asked, reaching out to undo my pants.

Fuck, she was gorgeous. Her hair tied long down her back. The rest of her bare. Perfect. From her silvery integrations to her pale, creamy skin. Those soft, small breasts with the rosy nipples, her narrow waist, broad hips, needy pussy.

I licked my lips, remembering her taste. My fangs

seeped their serum and I tasted it on my tongue. Sharp, dark flavor coated my palate and it made my cock swell. My inner Hyperion knew it was time, that there would be no holding back. That I would finally sink my fangs into my perfect mate and make her mine.

"I will claim you, Gwen." I moved her hands away as I opened the clasp on my pants myself. "There's just one small thing." Pushing the fabric down below my hips, I let my cock finally spring free. "Well, not a small thing."

Gwen's eyes dropped to my cock and I watched her response as it grew. And grew. My mating cock was ready to claim. To fuck. To fill. To finish.

Gwen

HOLY SHIT. Like, seriously, holy shit. Mak's cock was hard. And big. And long. And thick. And getting harder. And bigger. And longer. And thicker.

"Um, I don't remember it being that big," I said, staring. Ogling. Clenching my pussy in anticipation.

"This is what I wanted to tell you about," Mak said and I glanced up at him. "You know about the Hyperion bite while mating, but I never told you about the Forsian mating cock."

Mak didn't need to grip the base to keep it upright and aiming right at me. No, the base of it was big, wide, like ridiculously so. Like porn star dildo size. A deep ruddy red, there were thick, bulging veins that ran up the impressive length. And the head, wow. It was broad, flared and I whimpered knowing it would slide over every single hot button I had inside me. It had taken a lot of work to get him inside me the first time; I'd been on top and I'd had to work myself up and down, taking my time to open for him.

But this...

I squirmed on the bed, my thighs slick with my need. That serum injection had been like a drug, an arousal hit unlike I'd ever felt before. My breasts became tender and achy, my nipples hard points. My pussy ached and clenched, eager to be filled. My clit swelled, became more sensitive and I knew I could come if Mak gave it just the slightest bit of attention.

But I hadn't imagined... a mating cock.

"So it's just bigger. Okay, I can handle that."

With a hand placed between my breasts, he pushed me back. I fell onto the bed as he loomed over me. His hand grasped his huge Forsian cock and began to stroke. "It's not just bigger. When a Forsian claims his mate, he slides his cock nice and deep—taking the time to get all of it inside her pussy—and then it locks in place."

I frowned, but it was hard to follow what he was saying completely because he was gorgeous. A huge hulk of a male, his rippled chest bare and he was gripping a huge cock. His pants were open for it to jut out. The look of him was... virile. Arousing. He was so... male and he made all my female parts weep for him.

"Did you say lock?" I didn't see any kind of Hive integration on his cock—and I'd had a chance to look at it *very* up close.

"It swells, catches inside your pussy. I'll remain inside you until I'm done, female. Until I fill you with my seed. Until you are mine completely."

I pushed up to my elbows, watching as a drop of pre-cum slipped from the small slit. "For how long?"

"Until the Forsian mating is done," he replied. He pushed off his pants, stepped out of them and climbed onto the bed. I couldn't help but watch his cock as it aimed right for me. I gulped.

"And how long is that?" I asked.

"Hours."

"Hours," I repeated on a squeak. "Won't you get blue balls or something?"

He glanced down at himself between us, then at me. "I do not know this term, but I think I understand. I will come many times inside your perfect pussy, filling you with my seed."

"But don't you need a break or something to, you know... recharge?"

His hand came up, stroked my hair, his thumb brushing over my cheek. "I will remain hard for the duration. I will be able to please you... for hours."

For hours.

"I might not die from the bite, but I may die from pleasure."

He growled, his face all of a sudden fierce. "No dying."

Shit, right. Bad joke. "I'm sorry. I didn't mean to make you upset or scared. Or freaked out. I just wanted you to see that there's nothing to worry about."

"Besides a red ass," he countered, his gaze lowering to my mouth.

"What were you saying about lasting for hours?"

If he didn't like the joke about dying, then I didn't like the joke about him spanking me. I wasn't going to tell him that, surprisingly, it was really hot. Or maybe it was the serum making me think that. He'd spanked me before, yet perhaps he'd have to do it again to see. I squirmed at the thought.

The corner of his mouth tipped up. "We will fuck continuously until the claiming is done. You may pass out from the strength of your orgasms, but don't worry, I will wait for you to awaken for more."

"Oh god," I whispered. *Pass out from pleasure? Bring it.* "Okay. I'm ready."

He studied me, his dark eyes meeting mine. "No, you're not."

I frowned. "I am."

He slowly shook his head. "If you are talking in sentences, then you are not ready."

He kissed me then, holding my head in place with his palm. Gently, sweetly and almost reverently.

After the wall-banging sex we'd had before, this was... tame. Gentle. This was about so much more than sex. God, his touch was tender. Gentle.

Reverent.

Tears were gathering as my heart swelled painfully in my chest, the rapid beating like a hummingbird's wings against my ribs. "I love you, Mak." His entire body went still, as if I'd frozen him in place. Shit. Maybe I should have kept my stupid, needy mouth shut.

He lifted his head, stared down at me in silence.

Yep. Should have kept the weak, emotional, *needy* female parts of me to myself.

I turned my head away, embarrassed now, but his growl of warning came seconds before his huge hand cupped the side of my face, turning me back to face him.

"No. Do not hide from me."

I stared up into his eyes, drowning. Lost. He was my everything. "I'm sorry. I shouldn't have said that. You don't have to—"

"Be quiet, female. I know the human word—love. But that is not what I feel for you. That word means nothing, mate. I live and die to please you, to protect you, to ensure your happiness. Your pain is my agony. I am yours, Gwendolyn of Earth. Yours. I give myself to you, pledge myself to you and only you. I will never leave your side."

The tears slipped free and he bent down, kissing the wetness from my temples, tasting my pain. I couldn't seem to make them stop, like he'd broken a dam inside me and years of loneliness poured out.

I wrapped my arms around him, pulled him to me. Kissed him for the first time with every single cell in my body loving him, wanting only him. Welcoming him.

His lips were only sweet for a few seconds and then it turned carnal. Oh yeah, lots of tongue and, god, did he taste good.

His lips moved to my jaw, then my neck, his teeth grazing over my pulse, then lower. "Here, mate. I will claim you forever." He nipped at my skin and my back arched up off the bed, eager. "I will bite you here when I'm buried deep in your pussy, my cum coating you, filling you."

I whimpered and angled my head. He could do it now and I'd be fine. But no.

His mouth continued a downward path to my breasts, taking one taut nipple into his mouth, suckling, laving and tugging on it. I knew my nipples to be sensitive, but not like this. My hands tangled in his hair as I held him in place. If he kept at it, I might actually come.

Again, no. He moved to the other one, licking and

kissing my skin on the way. He only shifted from one breast to the other until I was writhing beneath him and begging for more.

Only then did he kiss his way to my navel, then lower, using his broad shoulders to part my legs and settle between. Large palms cupped the insides of my thighs and spread me wider as he put his mouth on me.

I bowed off the bed at the first touch of his talented tongue to my clit. "Mak!" I cried.

"Sensitive," he murmured.

"I'm going to come," I told him. Just one more brush of his tongue and I'd go over. The serum was *that* good. Before Mak, I'd never been able to come from oral sex alone, but with him—his mouth, tongue, lips—wow.

"Not yet."

"Not yet?" I asked. Sweat coated my skin and I couldn't remain still, although his grip on my thighs held me in place. In fact, he curved his palms to cup my butt and I wasn't going anywhere. Immobile just where he wanted me.

"You'll come when I sink my cock into you."

And I wanted him right where he was. Between my thighs, his face hovering just over me. I could feel his warm breath. "In me. Please."

"You beg so sweetly."

Frustrated, I used all my strength to flip us over, although all that did was have me straddling his head, his hands still cupping me. This time, his mouth was inches beneath my pussy.

"This way works, too," he commented, lowering me down so he could suck one lower lip into his mouth, then the other before his tongue stiffened and he circled my weeping entrance. Prodded it with a promise of what was to come. But that mating cock was so, so much bigger.

My head fell back and I felt my hair brush over my back, my skin so sensitive. He was incredibly skilled at bringing me to the brink, but not over.

"Mak... I need. God, now. Hurry. Must—more."

"There we go. Mindless," he said when he flipped us over once again. He crawled up my body so he hovered over me again. This time I felt his cock prodding at my entrance, slipping over my dripping folds. I was wet from Mak's mouth and from my own need. My body was primed, well-lubricated for the big cock it was about to take. Perhaps the serum helped with that, doing something to my body to make me wetter than I'd ever been in my life.

"Will you, Gwendolyn from Earth, become my claimed mate for all eternity?"

Oh. This moment was a big deal. It was hard for the haze of lust to clear enough to think, but I knew what he was asking. There would be no going back after this. Not just the fact that I'd never be able to consider any other cock ever again, but any other male.

No. Mak was mine. The one for me. The only one.

"Yes, Mak. I want to be your claimed mate. Bite me. Fuck me. Do the Forsian lock thing. Now."

Lifting my hips, the broad head of his cock pressed against my entrance and nudged inside.

Big. Fucking big.

"Oh god."

He leaned onto one forearm, keeping his weight off of me. His other hand cupped my breast, tugged at the nipple. "Oh," I gasped.

He slipped in a little further.

"Good girl. You feel so good. Perfect. You were made for me."

He crooned to me, whispered endearments, encouragement, sexy talk that had him sliding into me, filling me more and more and more until there was no doubt we were one.

I bent my knees and put my feet on the bed at his hips, lifted up and he slid a little deeper.

Mak was breathing hard, sweat dotted his brow. I could tell he was holding back, at least for now until I had taken him all, until I had adjusted to his huge, huge cock.

His hand cupped the back of my knee, pushed it wide and then up, opening me to him even more.

I gasped when he slid in all the way. He bottomed out, that blunt crown nudging my womb. I had no doubt if I weren't on birth control, I'd be pregnant by morning.

"You feel so fucking good," he growled. "Oh shit, I can feel myself getting even bigger."

"The base," I gasped, feeling it grow, spread even further.

Mak pulled back, but only moved about an inch, but didn't retreat any further. "That's it. We're locked together. Are you all right?"

He stroked my face again in the way I liked as he looked down at me. So intent, concerned.

I rippled around him, still adjusting to being opened up so much. It didn't hurt, but if he didn't start to move, I was going to go insane.

"Mak, please," I whimpered, trying to lift up to make him fuck me.

He slid back in that little bit.

"Yes!" I cried, and grabbed at his lower back.

He fucked me slowly, getting used to being so... together. This wasn't wild and crazy, but close. Personal. Us.

When he pulled back and slid deep again, I came. My head arched back, my cry filling the room. The pleasure of it went on and on as Mak continued to slide in and out.

"Gwen," he shouted, lowering his head into the crook of my neck. I heard him groan, "Mine," just before his teeth—his fangs—penetrated the spot where my neck and shoulder met.

I screamed, the searing hit of the bite was replaced immediately with a different kind of burn from the serum.

It was like instant pleasure, so intense I came. It wasn't my clit that was the epicenter of my pleasure, but Mak himself. I felt his pleasure as he felt mine.

"Yes, god yes!" I cried as I let it wash over me.

His hand tightened on my knee as his teeth remained embedded deep in my flesh, just like his cock. I felt the heat of his seed fill me, slip around our joining and escape. There was just no room for all of it. No room for anything, no thought, no sound, no feeling but him. But us.

I had no sense of time, but Mak lifted his head, licked at the wound. It felt sore, tender, but only for a moment. My eyes blinked open and I saw him studying the mark as if I'd been wrong and there was still a chance I might die.

I only felt pleasure, felt Mak deep—so deep—inside me.

"More," I begged, tugging him back down with my hand cupped behind his head.

"More," Mak growled, grinning. His fangs were gone. He kissed me and fucked me some more. When he pulled back this time, the mating cock somehow allowed for more movement, more friction and he took advantage.

Grabbing my ankles, he lifted them to his shoulders for a more direct thrust. He took me that way until I came, delirious with pleasure. It never ended, but built higher and higher. I wasn't sure how he'd flipped me onto my hands and knees with his cock stuck inside me, but he did. Then fucked me some more. He came again, more seed, more pleasure.

It blended together in a sweaty, sticky, loving mess until Mak had me in front of him, like we were two spoons in a drawer as he slowly took me once more. I did pass out then, for I woke up with his hand cupping my breast as he continued to rock his hips. This time it was a slow fuck, gentle and almost like a break. But we were *still* connected.

"Will the pleasure ever stop?" I whispered, moving into the feel of him.

"Hours, mate. Hours."

EPILOGUE

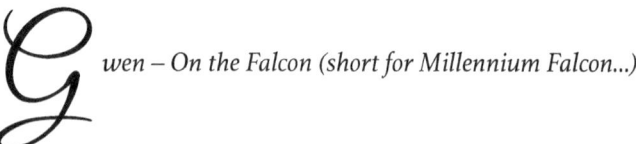

Gwen – On the Falcon (short for Millennium Falcon...)

"You'll need to put your hair up in cinnamon buns over your ears," Kristin said.

I laughed and Mak looked at me, confused. I'd told him all about *Star Wars* when I named our ship, but he got caught up on what the purpose of an Earth movie was before I could get into a lot of detail.

"Mak doesn't look furry enough to be Chewbacca, but he certainly snarls a lot," Rachel added. She was bouncing her son on her hip and he was happily chewing on a fistful of Rachel's long hair, slobbering all over his hand... and her.

Babies. Adorable. But maybe a bit too slobbery for me.

I smiled, looked to Mak and ran my hand down his cheek. "I like it when you snarl."

We were in our ship's central area, sharing a vid screen

call with our friends on The Colony. Everyone was in the governor's quarters, getting together so we could all visit.

It had been two weeks since the battle in the caves. Two weeks since all imminent Colony threats from the Hive were over. The Colony was at peace and it showed in the smiles and relaxed looks on all of their faces.

Maxim, his second, Ryston, and Rachel were there. The governor took their baby boy, Max, from his mother and the little boy curled into his father, happy to be in his arms. Maximus Rone was a very happy, chubby, perfect little creature. From what Rachel had said, they didn't have juniors or thirds or whatever on Prillon, but the Prillon warriors liked the idea of him being named after his primary father. And Rachel had privately confessed to me that she loved Maximus in the movie, *Gladiator*. Win-win. I couldn't argue with that. With dark hair like Rachel, gorgeous caramel skin and a fierce, stubborn temper like his second father, it seemed the baby had inherited something from each of them. No doubt he'd be big and fierce like all three of his parents.

Mak smiled. "Me, too."

"You're sure you want to roam the universe with Mak? I mean, just the two of you, alone on a spaceship..." Kristin said. Their little girl, Tia, was resting on her shoulder, Kristin patting her little upturned butt. With her pixie haircut and bright blonde hair, she and her daughter looked nearly identical. Except little Tia's eyes, when she looked at me, were a rich, golden amber. Just like Hunt's.

Kristin glanced up over her shoulder at her mates, Tyran and Hunt, who stood behind her chair. "You should come home to The Colony and start making babies. We shouldn't have to suffer alone on this planet. We need all the estrogen we can get around here."

Out of the vid screen's view, Mak squeezed my hand. We didn't know if I could get pregnant with his child. It hadn't happened, no doubt partly due to the birth control shot I had requested the moment I'd arrived on The Colony. And it had only been a few weeks since I'd called Mak's name in the fighting pit. Not very long at all, yet so much had happened.

I wasn't ready to be a mother. Wasn't sure I would ever be ready. And Mak? He was okay with that, content to enjoy his time with me. *Practicing.*

For now, I was really, *really* enjoying all the practice. Several times a day. Yes, my mate was *very* lusty. And I didn't mind his huge cock either.

"Just think, mates," Kristin continued. "If we had a spaceship all to ourselves, I'd be pregnant again, already."

Tyran arched one brow, crossed his arms over his chest. "Mate, we do not need a spaceship to get you pregnant. We just need you alone." He continued to stare at her and I could tell they were doing some kind of mental talking through their collars.

"Oh boy," Rachel said, laughing as she walked over to Kristin. "Here. I'll take Tia."

As soon as Rachel had the baby, Tyran leaned down and scooped up Kristin, tossed her over his shoulder. "Say goodbye to your friends," he said, turning toward the doorway I could see in the background.

"Bye, Gwen. Talk again soon!" Kristin yelled through laughter. I had no idea what kind of naughtiness she'd been sending her mates, but neither of them looked back as they carried her out of the room. The door slid closed behind them and all was quiet for a moment.

I was smiling now. "I'm guessing she totally deserved that. "

The door slid open and Rezzer and Caroline stepped inside, each carrying one of their newborn twins.

"Oh my god, CJ! You should be in bed, woman!" Rachel chastised her, but CJ rolled her eyes.

"And miss my chance to say thank you? No way." She turned to me, her infant in her arms, and wiped a tear from her eye. "Thank you, Gwen. Mak. I can't even tell you what it means to us that he's dead and gone." I knew who she was talking about. We all did. Nexus 4. I hadn't stayed around to make sure the Atlans in the cave finished him off. Didn't need to add more gory memories to the stockpile in my mind. But I was glad he was dead. Very, very glad.

"I tore him into pieces and burned him to ash, mate. He will never harm you or our children again." Rezzer's face contorted, his eyes glowing with a partial change into his beast. But he controlled his emotions quickly, as the infant wrapped in a fluffy white blanket reached for his face. Tiny fingers grabbed at his jaw and Rezzer transformed from angry warrior to smitten daddy in the blink of an eye. I had no idea if he held his daughter, CJ—for Caroline Junior—or RJ—for Rezzer Junior, but it didn't matter. The twins were safe and warm and surrounded by people who not only loved them, but would die to protect them.

Rachel kissed baby Tia, who was reaching for baby Max. Babies loved other babies. Who knew? It struck me as odd and endearing. When little golden-headed Tia leaned over, open-mouthed, to 'kiss' Max on his head, my heart skipped a beat and I finally understood the reality of being a warrior, knew I'd never stop. Not until every last Nexus unit was dead. Every Hive Soldier either freed or put out of his misery. For that kiss. Those smiles. The innocence in those bright little eyes.

Mak pulled me into his side and wrapped an arm around me as if he could feel my emotional turmoil. The protective instincts surging through me weren't bad... but they were *strong.* Unexpectedly so. I was stronger, faster, more deadly than anyone on the planet. I could get close to the Nexus units. I knew now that I'd need Mak's help finishing them off, but he seemed more than happy to have my back.

And I had people I loved now. People who mattered to me. A family on The Colony that needed me and my mate to protect them. Fight for them. So I would. I'd fight to my dying breath to protect what I saw in that room. What I knew existed on countless homes on hundreds of worlds.

I leaned into Mak, my entire body overflowing with love and trust and gratitude that he was mine.

"Mak, I'm sure you'll be pleased to hear the final report." Maximus was back in governor mode, which seemed oddly out of place with a small baby in his arms.

Mak grunted a vague reply at the governor's words.

"Krael's dead. None of us would have let him off this planet alive. We—Ryston, Tyran, Hunt, Marz, Vance and the other Prillons—all agreed we wouldn't give him an opportunity to escape. Justice has been served with him."

I watched as the remainder of the men in the room nodded.

"The mineral extraction plan has been terminated. New protocols have been put in place to protect future resources. The schematics and details on that ship outlined their plan.

It should be easy for our warriors here on The Colony to eliminate any further threat to the Coalition. At least for now."

"You are at peace," Mak said. "Good."

The governor nodded, then glanced down at his baby. "We are."

He looked straight at the vid screen, at us. "You two are welcome here, any time. You are family."

Having the governor say that meant a lot. I hadn't been the easiest resident and neither had Mak. "That's kind of you and we will keep that in mind," I said.

"But you'll roam the universe in your stolen Hive ship and hunt for the other Nexus units."

"That's off the record, Maxim. We'll keep in touch," I said.

"Promise?" Rachel asked.

"I promise."

She nodded.

I looked to Mak. Smiled. All was right with our world. *Our world* was this ship. Each other. The universe.

We'd go visit on The Colony, someday. For now, I was content with Mak.

Happy.

Loved.

Free.

And I wouldn't have it any other way.

A SPECIAL THANK YOU TO MY READERS...

Want more? I've got *hidden* bonus content on my web site *exclusively* for those on my mailing list.

If you are already on my email list, you don't need to do a thing! Simply scroll to the bottom of my newsletter emails and click on the *super-secret* link.

Not a member? What are you waiting for? In addition to ALL of my bonus content (great new stuff will be added regularly) you will be the first to hear about my newest release the second it hits the stores—AND you will get a free book as a special welcome gift.

Sign up now! http://freescifiromance.com

FIND YOUR INTERSTELLAR MATCH!

YOUR mate is out there. Take the test today and discover your perfect match. Are you ready for a sexy alien mate (or two)?

VOLUNTEER NOW!

interstellarbridesprogram.com

DO YOU LOVE AUDIOBOOKS?

Grace Goodwin's books are now available as audiobooks...everywhere.

LET'S TALK SPOILER ROOM!

Interested in joining my **Sci-Fi Squad**? Meet new like-minded sci-fi romance fanatics and chat with Grace! Get excerpts, cover reveals and sneak peeks before anyone else. Be part of a private Facebook group that shares pictures and fun news! Join here:

https://www.facebook.com/groups/scifisquad/

***

Want to talk about Grace Goodwin books with others? Join the **SPOILER ROOM** and spoil away! Your GG BFFs are waiting! (And so is Grace)

Join here:

https://www.facebook.com/groups/ggspoilerroom/

GET A FREE BOOK!

Join my mailing list to be the first to know of new releases, free books, special prices and other author giveaways.

http://freescifiromance.com

ALSO BY GRACE GOODWIN

Interstellar Brides® Program

Mastered by Her Mates

Assigned a Mate

Mated to the Warriors

Claimed by Her Mates

Taken by Her Mates

Mated to the Beast

Tamed by the Beast

Mated to the Vikens

Her Mate's Secret Baby

Mating Fever

Her Viken Mates

Fighting For Their Mate

Her Rogue Mates

Claimed By The Vikens

The Commanders' Mate

Matched and Mated

Hunted

Viken Command

Interstellar Brides® Program: The Colony

Surrender to the Cyborgs

Mated to the Cyborgs

Cyborg Seduction

Her Cyborg Beast

Cyborg Fever

Rogue Cyborg

Cyborg's Secret Baby

Interstellar Brides® Program: The Virgins

The Alien's Mate

Claiming His Virgin

His Virgin Mate

His Virgin Bride

Interstellar Brides® Program: Ascension Saga

Ascension Saga, book 1

Ascension Saga, book 2

Ascension Saga, book 3

Trinity: Ascension Saga - Volume 1

Ascension Saga, book 4

Ascension Saga, book 5

Ascension Saga, book 6

Faith: Ascension Saga - Volume 2

Ascension Saga, book 7

Ascension Saga, book 8

Ascension Saga, book 9

Destiny: Ascension Saga - Volume 3

Other Books

Their Conquered Bride

Wild Wolf Claiming: A Howl's Romance

ABOUT GRACE

Grace Goodwin is a *USA Today* and international bestselling author of Sci-Fi & Paranormal romance. Grace believes all women should be treated like royalty, in the bedroom and out of it, and writes love stories where men know how to make their women feel pampered, protected and very well taken care of. Grace hates the snow, loves the mountains (yes, that's a problem) and wishes she could simply download the stories out of her head instead of being forced to type them out. Grace lives in the western US and is a full-time writer, an avid reader and an admitted caffeine addict. She is active on Facebook and loves to chat with readers and fellow sci-fi fanatics.

All of Grace's books can be read as sexy, stand-alone adventures. But be careful, she likes her heroes hot and her love scenes hotter. You have been warned...

www.gracegoodwin.com
gracegoodwinauthor@gmail.com

www.ingramcontent.com/pod-product-compliance
Lightning Source LLC
LaVergne TN
LVHW011825060526
838200LV00053B/3900